MEGAN'S MATES

SHIFTER MENAGE ROMANCE

ANN GIMPEL

Edited by
ANGELA KELLY
Illustrated by
FIONA JAYDE

CONTENTS

MEGAN'S MATES

WOLF CLAN SHIFTERS, BOOK TWO

Shifter Ménage Romance
By
Ann Gimpel

One virgin + two wolf shifters = e-reader ecstasy

BOOK DESCRIPTION: MEGAN'S MATES

Calgary, Alberta 1936

After witnessing what might've been a murder, Megan is frantic to escape the Garden of Eden cult, so she catches the night train north out of town. Her lifetime commitment to the cult may well be her death sentence, but she's not sticking around to let them frame her.

Wolf shifters, Les and Karl, eke out a primitive existence on the flanks of the Canadian Rockies. Between Hunters who want to kill them and a wildfire raging out of control, they're glad when Jed, their clan leader, shows up. And even more delighted when they see who's in his car.

Jed's mate, Alice, spied Megan by the side of the road looking lost and desperate and offered her a ride. Before Jed's car even stops rolling, Les and Karl know she's their mate. So skittish she's barely willing to exit the car, Megan busies herself helping Jed and his pack mates unload supplies. Can Les and Karl convince her to join her life to theirs? If she does, will the risks she faced as a cult member pale in comparison to being mated to shifters?

CHAPTER 1

utumn, 1936

The swish of tires on wet pavement drove Megan deeper into the shadows of a band of oak trees. She pulled her black wool cloak tighter against her body and set her teeth to keep them from chattering. Maybe running away from the Garden of Eden cult hadn't been such a hot idea, but staying didn't work either. Not after what she'd witnessed last night.

When she'd joined the group two years ago, they'd been warm and welcoming. The rituals were a bit risqué, but harmless all in all. She squeezed her eyes shut to block out the image of a cheering mob that had segued from chanting while scantily clad to blood sacrifice. Exposing her body was one thing, a thirst for human blood quite another...

She pried her eyes open. No one would save her except herself, and there wasn't much she could do by playing ostrich. Escape was essential. The only thing that mattered. Never mind she'd be walking away from what little she owned since her things were in one of the cult's many apartments.

Megan took another step backward. One boot sank into sticky mud, and cold water ran into it. Reality hit home and terrified her. She couldn't go back to work. Nearly everyone she knew at the insurance exchange was related to the cult in some way. Or to another similar group. Occult fervor had risen during the twenties in the wake of World War I. By the middle of the nineteen thirties, it had a well-established toehold. Fascination with the supernatural ran high and had grown like an out-of-control weed. Most spiritual cults were rooted in the States, but it hadn't taken long before Canadians picked up the banner, enthralled by the unseen world.

Despite Megan's best efforts, shudders racked her body, and her teeth banged against one another uncontrollably. October in Calgary meant the air was dry and crisp. She'd seen frost on the roofs this morning. Tonight would likely be another freeze. It didn't take much of an imagination to realize winter would set in soon.

Somehow, she'd sat at her desk all day. When co-workers commented she seemed subdued, she'd just said she wasn't feeling well. It was the only way she'd gotten out of mandatory attendance at tonight's cult meeting. Midday, she'd slipped out of the office and stopped by the bank. Closing her account would've engendered suspicion, so she'd withdrawn two hundred dollars, half of what she had saved. Even that earned her a stern lecture from one of the bank vice presidents. Likely afraid she'd fallen for a swindle from some fast-talking salesman, he drew her into a side office intent on discovering why she needed such a vast sum of money. Megan rolled her eyes at the memory. She'd fabricated a story about a mythical aunt who had unexpected medical bills.

"Yes, and I'm wasting precious time standing here," she muttered, the words barely discernable against her chattering teeth. If she was going to follow through with the plan she'd hatched during the day, she needed to be out of town and well-hidden before someone looked for her. If she got really lucky, that wouldn't be until after she didn't show up for work tomorrow.

Aw crap! They might send someone to my place tonight to see if I need anything.

That last thought galvanized her into action. Megan broke into a shambling trot and ducked into a coffee shop. She needed something hot to drink, and then she'd head for the train station and catch the evening express north toward Edmonton.

"Looking pretty wet there, hon." A smiling waitress hustled over to her. "We're closing soon, but I can get you some soup."

"Just coffee," Megan managed. "And I promise I'll drink it fast."

The waitress, a buxom blonde with gray roots, cocked her head to one side. "You okay, sweetie?" Her brown eyes flickered kindly.

"Fine." She dug a nickel out of a pocket. "Here's for the coffee. I like it black."

The waitress frowned and then shrugged. "It's six cents now, but seeing as how we're just going to toss what's left in the pot, keep your money. Looks as if you need it worse than we do."

Tears threatened at the woman's unexpected thoughtfulness. Megan blinked them back and murmured, "Thank you." She sank into a red leather padded chair at the counter and waited while the waitress poured steaming liquid into a heavy, white ceramic mug. The heated crockery felt heavenly when she cradled it between her hands. The coffee burned her tongue, but the jolt from the caffeine was instantaneous and welcome.

Megan glanced at her watch. How had it gotten to be nine p.m.? Her train left in an hour. The station was a thirty minute walk, and she needed time to purchase a ticket once she got there. She didn't have extra money to waste on streetcars or taxis. Setting her cup down, she nodded at the waitress and hurried out of the café. The streets weren't exactly deserted, so she pulled the sodden wool of her cloak's hood over her bright hair. She didn't want to have to explain why she hadn't been at the meeting if anyone recognized her. After all, her excuse had been she was too sick to leave her home that night, and it would be blown to hell if anyone spotted her wandering around in marginal weather.

Stop that! She lectured herself. *Everyone else is at cult headquarters. No one's out and about who might recognize me.*

Brave words. Too bad I don't believe them.

Her heart thudded so hard, she was afraid everyone she passed could hear it. Megan counted off blocks as she walked through the heart of Calgary's business district. Her wet sock squished in her boot. She wished she had time to take it off and wring it out. Another café, this one advertising it stayed open until ten, looked inviting, but she walked on by.

I'll take care of my sock problem at the station. I'm cutting the timing close as it is.

Megan felt ill. The coffee she'd welcomed going down burned her stomach like acid. If she met up with anyone from the cult at the train station, she'd be finished. Cult members signed on for life. There weren't any early out clauses that she knew of. A tear dripped down one cheek; she brushed it aside. No point feeling sorry for herself. She'd made a bad decision and didn't have a fall-back position. No family to run home to—or call for help. They'd all died in the flu epidemic of 1918. She'd been seven at the time and had ended up in the Calgary orphanage.

"Even if I had relatives," she mumbled, "they'd be the last place I'd go. Wouldn't want to implicate them." There hadn't been anything truly wrong with the orphanage, but there hadn't been much right there, either. Megan understood perfectly why she'd been so attracted to the cult. For the first time in her twenty-five years, she felt as if she belonged somewhere. Like she had a family.

What a joke! Megan castigated herself for being a fool, and a gullible one at that, and then gave it up for wasted effort.

The station lights shone through ground fog that had misted out of nowhere during her flight across town. A few more steps and she pushed the door open, walking into warmth so welcome it took her breath away. She hadn't realized how cold she'd become. Not just body-cold. Her spirit was frozen to the core of her soul.

Megan gazed around the station. A few people milled about, but not many. Resolute now that she was here, she marched to an open ticket counter and said, "Edmonton, please. Economy coach."

The man didn't bother to look up. "How many?" In his fifties or sixties, he was rail thin with sparse, gray hair.

"Just me."

"Name?"

"Megan Galen."

His fingers shook as he wrote out her ticket. "That'll be a dollar-fifty, miss."

"Oh." She bit her lower lip and fished in her handbag.

He glanced at her, rheumy blue eyes shrewd. "You got a problem with that?"

Megan swallowed hard. It went against the grain, but she spoke up for herself. "Since you asked, yes I do. I don't have much, and I thought the advertised fare was a dollar. I, um, called today and asked about it."

He shrugged. "You got a buck?" She held it up so he could see. "Okay, missy. Here's your ticket." He stamped it and held it out to her, but Megan was so nonplussed he'd tried to overcharge her, she didn't reach for it.

"Ain't you going to take your ticket?" He sounded annoyed.

"Yeah, sure." She pushed her money under the bars and grasped the ticket, tucking it into a pocket.

"Gate seven. She boards in twenty minutes."

Megan scuttled away, not wanting to deal with the clerk who'd tried to cheat her. If she wouldn't have said anything, he would've pocketed the extra fifty cents. Outrage flooded her and left a bitter taste at the back of her mouth. Someone really should report him.

Yes, someone should, but not me. The last thing I need is to draw attention to myself.

Following the signs, she settled in to wait near where the train would come and bent to unlace her boot. Her sock had soaked up most of the water. She wrung out what she could and put it back on before the wool cooled off and turned clammy. Some strands of her white-blonde hair had escaped from beneath her hood. She tucked them back out of sight and drew in a shuddery breath. Fifteen more minutes and she'd be safe on the train. Well, *maybe* safe, though it seemed unlikely she'd run into any Garden of Edeners on the night train to Edmonton.

She'd studied maps during the day and decided to get off at Red Deer. Buying a ticket all the way to Edmonton was a hedge in case anyone tried to find out where she'd gone. From Red Deer, hopefully she could hitch a ride west into some of the smaller communities dotting the Rockies. Maybe, if she was really lucky, she could land a job before her money ran out. Insofar as she knew, cult activities were limited outside major cities.

Wonder how much trouble they're going to go to in order to find me?

The loudspeaker announced her train. After a final, furtive glance around the station, Megan strode toward the door and out onto the platform. The steam engine's headlamp lit the night. With a whoosh and a roar, the train clattered to a halt. She waited until a flood of travelers disembarked, then she climbed the steps and found her way to a nearly deserted coach.

Her seat was soft and the train car warm. Her eyelids grew heavy before the train even pulled out of the station. Megan pinched her hands. Sleeping, at least until they got underway, wasn't an option. She had to stay alert and keep an eye on the few passengers entering her car.

It wasn't easy. She'd barely slept the night before as her mind replayed the horror of a man she'd known and respected chopping off two of his fingers while lost in cult-driven zeal. If it had just been him, acting by himself, it might've been one thing, but hundreds of other cult members were screeching, cheering, and egging him on. They'd put his fingers into a brass bowl and used the blood to try to lure a spirit guide.

When their efforts didn't seem to be working, the man twisted and plunged his knife into the nearest bystander—a woman Megan knew from work—screeching, "Blood! We need more blood."

The woman fell to the floor shrieking and clutching a belly spewing blood. Rather than summoning aid, the other cult members sank into a pitched argument about the trouble they'd get into if anyone found out.

Horrified and disbelieving—and with the woman's piteous cries for help echoing in her ears—Megan excused herself, barely making it to the ladies' room before her stomach rebelled. She hadn't returned, but the cult was so high on bloodlust, she figured no one noticed her absence. She'd placed an anonymous call to the Police from a corner pay phone before scurrying home and locking her doors.

Showing up at work today, so she could buy herself enough time to flee, had taken every shred of strength she possessed. As the minutes ticked by, she felt worse and worse. Why wasn't the train leaving? Had someone from the cult figured things out? Even worse, had they pinned last night's attack on her?

Were the police on their way right now to pick her up and throw her in jail? Bile splashed the back of her throat, and she fought against the urge to vomit. She had to stay in her seat. *Had to.*

Finally, after she was so racked with nerves she wanted to scream, the wheels squealed against the rails, and the train chugged northward. Despite her grim imaginings, her car was still mostly empty. As she sank deeper into her seat and drew her hood low over her eyes, Megan dared to let herself hope. She'd made it this far. Maybe, just maybe, she'd escape to start a new life.

One where she'd make better choices.

~

THE PHONE JANGLED AGAIN. Loud and strident, it made Les' sensitive lupine hearing ache. It took him a moment to realize he needed his human form to make the noise go away. He'd tried to ignore the damned thing, but whoever was calling wouldn't give up. Every time he ventured near the house, it was ringing. With an aggravated growl, he commanded his body to shift.

As soon as he had feet rather than paws, he strode through the door of his cabin deep in the woods, jaw tight with annoyance. The remote location a few miles outside Rocky Mountain House often lost phone service for long periods of time.

"Yes and too bad this isn't one of them," he muttered, snatched up the receiver, and barked, "Yes, I'm here."

"It's about damned time. I've been trying to get hold of you for days."

Les' eyes widened. "Jed?"

"Who the hell else?"

Les brayed laughter. "Good point. It's not as if very many people have this number. What's up, boss? I thought you were coming my way months ago. The boys and I wondered what happened."

"Now that I have your attention, hang up." Jed's voice held a sharp edge that Les remembered all too well. "We'll do this a more private way."

"You got it." Les dropped the black receiver back into place. He kicked the door shut to keep the cold breeze out. It didn't bother him as a wolf, but he was naked, and the air had a chill edge to it. He trotted into the bedroom and had begun to dress when Jed's voice sounded in his mind.

"Where the hell have you been? I've been trying to reach you for a week."

Les sank onto the bed and pulled a quilt over his still-bare legs as he considered where to start. Jed was clan leader for wolf shifters. He needed all the information Les could provide. *"First off, we're all still okay."*

"That's a relief. When I couldn't raise you, I was afraid Hunters had killed everyone. Made me half-crazy not to know anything. Anyway, we pulled into Calgary last night, so I'm finally close enough to use telepathy."

"Is your new mate with you?"

"Affirmative. Bron, Terin, and Alice are with me." Jed blew out a breath. *"You may have heard through the grapevine, we'd originally decided to come north as part of our wedding trip, but Hunters nabbed half a dozen of us in northern California. It took a major offensive to free our people. Even so, we lost a couple."*

Les nodded, and then realized Jed couldn't see him. *"Yes, I know. We've had problems of our own. Hunters almost got your cousins, Ron and Chris. We killed them, and I'm still waiting for the fallout on that one since we also killed the whole posse that came afterward, hunting for their fallen companions. All five of them."*

"How many total? Was there any choice?" Jed's voice was stern as he peppered Les with questions.

"Seven. No, no choice." Anger tightened Les' muscles. He'd like to kill every goddamned Hunter in the universe, but he wasn't about to tell Jed that. And there hadn't been any choice, not really. They'd been surrounded. The only thing that saved them was taking a firm offensive position.

Jed broke into Les' thoughts. *"What'd you do with the bodies?"*

"Don't worry, boss. No one will ever find them. We dragged them to the very bottom of a cave system where there's a vent to an upper cave and burned them."

"How long ago?"

Les thought about it. He'd spent much of the last month as a wolf, which skewed his time sense. *"Maybe a week."*

"You still haven't told me why you weren't answering your phone."

"We've all been in our wolf forms. There's a fire burning out of control between our pack and the crest of the Rockies. A couple of the cabins farther west incinerated—"

"Humph," Jed interrupted, obviously not concerned about an out-of-control wildfire. *"Any of you find mates yet?"*

"What do you think? It's not as if the odds are in our favor."

"Maybe Alice can change that. Women trust her. She's actually scared up three mates since she joined Bron, Terin, and me." A hesitation. *"How close did you say that fire was?"*

"My cabin's not in any immediate danger. It's fall and I'm expecting it to rain soon." Les scratched at month-old beard growth on his chin. *"It's pretty primitive here, boss. Nothing like your digs in Hollywood."*

A different voice sounded in his head, rich, vibrant, and definitely female. *"I've been listening in. Shameless of me not to have said something earlier. Don't worry about me. My life was a whole lot simpler before I met up with Jed and my other two mates. Besides, I'm looking forward to meeting the clan members here in Alberta."*

Les' mouth twitched into half a smile. *"You must be Alice. We've heard a lot about you. Are you really six feet tall?"*

Alice snorted, making Les wish he'd kept his mouth shut. After all, Alice was mated to his clan leader. *"How about if we leave the details open, and you can see for yourself when we get there? Jed says it's a four or five hour drive, and we should arrive sometime tomorrow. Is there anything we need to bring from the big city?"*

Les gazed around his one-bedroom cabin as if he expected a grocery list to materialize. He cleared his throat before remembering he didn't need his actual voice. *"Um, we've been pretty much living off the land this past month, so anything you bring would be welcome."*

"I get the picture." Jed broke in with a laugh. *"We'll fill up the trunk and the rest of the back seat."*

Les couldn't help himself. *"Who gets to sit next to Alice?"*

Female chuckling made his heart lighter than it had been in a long time.

"Oh, they fuss and snarl a bit, but they sort of take turns. It's nice actually, to have three doting mates."

"I'm sure it is." Les brushed a wave of sadness aside. He'd love to have a woman to fuss over, alongside Karl, his pack mate. They'd hunted for years for a female to grace their lives without success after their first mate died in childbirth in the 1600s. A few promising candidates crossed their path when they'd lived in Edmonton, but Hunters had driven them out of the city fifty years before.

"We'll be there by tomorrow afternoon." Jed's voice was gruff, and Les figured his clan leader could read his mind.

"I'll alert the troops, boss. Everyone will be really glad to see all of you. And to meet your mate."

Les waited, but a certain emptiness told him Jed had signed off. He shoved the quilt aside, finished dressing, and called Karl through their telepathic link. It didn't take long before paws scrabbled against the door, and Les remembered he'd shut it. By the time he crossed the small space and pulled the door open, Karl had found his human form and stood shivering, arms wrapped around his tall, spare frame. Black hair hung to his waist in tangles.

"Thanks. Damned cold out here." The wolf shifter bounded into the room, giving the door a shove as he passed through it. "What's up?"

"Jed's here." Les spread his arms wide and rolled his eyes. "Along with his lieutenants and their new mate. We've got to clean this place up."

"Why? It's always been good enough for us."

Les slugged him in the arm. "You weren't listening. Jed's *mate* will be here."

"Oh, I get it." Karl chortled, his dark eyes gleaming with glee. "Maybe if we didn't do anything, she'd take pity on us and—"

"Right. Find some clothes, and we'll get to work. I don't think Jed, Terin, or Bron will want their new mate waiting on the likes of us."

Karl sprinted for his sleeping alcove toward the rear of the log cabin's main room. Drawers banged open. "Fire's getting closer," he called over one shoulder. "Maybe it would be better for all of us to get together in Red Deer."

Les considered it. "Nope. Too soon since we axed those Hunters. That's where they were from—there and Edmonton. I don't want any friendly sheriff asking questions if they discover we live out here. Are you sure the fire's closer? Maybe the wind just shifted direction."

"It's definitely closer. The smoke's thicker, and I can actually hear it burning from the rise a couple miles west of here. At least my wolf can." Karl slid his legs into trousers and pulled a sweater over his head before shoving his feet into an ancient pair of sheepskin slippers. He turned to Les. "Where do you think we should start? Come to think of it, when do you want to alert the rest of the clan, or should I do that?"

"We can take care of that later tonight. How about if you work on the dishes? I'll sweep and get the kettle going for laundry."

Karl strode to the sink and pumped the handle for water. "Eww." He wrinkled his nose. "How long have these plates been here?"

"Does it matter?" Les lugged a large, cast iron kettle in through the back door and hefted it onto a wood-burning stove. He opened the firebox door, levered a pocket knife out of his pants, and started shaving tinder. "Let's warm some water. That should help." As he worked, Les dialed in his lupine senses and scented fresh air coming through the back door. It was indeed tinged with smoke. What bad timing for a major fire. If it drove them into one of the nearby towns, they'd risk discovery because Hunters could scent them.

"Les?"

He looked up from his half-built fire. "Um-hum."

"Maybe it's time to move on."

"No!" Les banged a fist down on his thigh. "I'm sick of running. If the fire gets this far, we'll come back when it's over and rebuild."

"But we'll never find a mate out here."

"Just do the damned dishes. We've got enough problems without adding to them."

CHAPTER 2

Megan didn't know what jarred her from sleep, but the train wasn't moving. Where were they? Her mind felt thick and stupid as she gazed blearily around the car. The conductor strode past. "Excuse me." Her voice came out as a barely audible croak. The conductor kept moving, so apparently he hadn't heard her. Megan cleared her throat and lurched to her feet. "Excuse me, sir."

The conductor had nearly reached the end of the car. He turned. "Miss?"

"Where are we, please?"

"Red Deer."

She pushed her way toward him, stumbling slightly. "I need to get off."

The conductor shook his head. "It's too late, miss. We'll be underway again in a minute or two."

It can't be too late. The next stop isn't for miles.

"Please let me past. My sister, she's sick."

"Well, why didn't you say so?" The conductor, a youngish man with kind, brown eyes, took her arm and led her to the coupling between the cars. Megan was almost down the steps when he said, "Wait a minute. Didn't your ticket say Edmonton?"

She stepped onto the platform and half-turned, shielding her face with her hood. "No, sir. You must have mistaken me for a different passenger." The train whistle nearly deafened her. Steam filled the air as the powerful engine cranked up. Seizing opportunity, Megan fled into the night.

It had taken the train four hours to get from Calgary to Red Deer, which meant it was closing on two in the morning. She'd assumed the remaining hours of darkness would give her an edge to travel farther west. If Garden of Edeners took the trouble to hunt her down, surely they'd limit themselves to bigger cities. Her goal was Rocky Mountain House. Hopefully, it would be large enough for her to find work but small enough the cult would never think to look for her there.

Guess I'll find out.

Megan tried to get her bearings. Thick fog gave things a surreal aspect, but at least it wasn't raining. Though the night air cleared her mind quickly, it still took half an hour to locate the main highway leading west out of town. Megan stared at the deserted road. She'd hoped to thumb a ride, but there wasn't any traffic. None at all.

After waiting a few minutes, she began walking. Staying near the town had obvious advantages, like renting a room to wait out the night, but she didn't want to be tempted to spend the money. Daylight brought its own set of problems. Better to put as much distance between herself and her old life as she could. Her boots were sturdy, and her wet sock had nearly dried from the heat of her body.

Megan fell into a loping stride. Her long legs ate up distance quickly, but she wasn't under any illusions she could walk the whole eighty miles to Rocky Mountain House. The terrain was mostly relatively flat farmland, but she'd still need a ride to accomplish her goal.

She'd been ambivalent about hitchhiking but hadn't found any other options. Buses didn't run outside the cities and renting a car was outside her meager means. Besides she didn't have a license and didn't drive very well. After she'd been walking for half an hour or so, lights flared from behind her, cutting through the misty fog. Megan wasn't certain a driver would even see her, dressed in black as she was, so she tossed her hood back to reveal her pale blonde locks. Surely they'd reflect in the car's headlamps. Resolutely, she stepped closer to the road and stuck out her thumb. Part of her was terrified the car would stop; another part was scared it wouldn't.

Got to get hold of myself. I should be able to tell if the driver means me harm.

Headlines of missing women flashed through her mind, but Megan ignored them and pasted a smile on her face. The driver could probably see her by now. At first, it seemed the car would pass her by, but then brakes squealed loudly and the vehicle, a late model sedan, backed up. She trotted to the passenger side. By the time she got there, the driver had leaned across the seat and rolled the window partway down.

Megan peered into the car and blew out a nervous breath. She'd hoped for a family, but the driver—a man—was the car's sole occupant. Illuminated in the glow from the dome light, he looked dangerous. Powerfully built, he might've been in his mid-thirties with cropped brown hair and dark blue eyes. There was a time she might have thought him handsome, but something told her getting in the car wasn't a good idea.

She backed away from the window. "Sorry," she mumbled. "I was hoping for a family I could hitch a ride with."

The emergency brake crackled as he pulled it into place. The driver door opened and slammed shut. Megan spun and ran into fields bordering the roadway, immediately blundering into a barbed wire fence.

"Miss. I'm not going to hurt you." The man's mellow baritone wasn't particularly reassuring.

She tugged at her cloak, but it was caught in the fence. The taste of fear, sharp and metallic, flooded her mouth. "Then why'd you get out of your car?"

"You looked like you were about to bolt. And you did. What happened? You caught in the farmer's fence?" Footsteps sounded on pavement and then were muffled as he worked his way to her side. "Here, let me help." He pulled a small flashlight out of a pocket and shone it on the fence. Nimble fingers plucked her wool cloak from where it was snagged. He stepped away from her as soon as she was free. "There. See. Not going to hurt you, but you might not be so lucky with the next car. Why the hell are you hitchhiking in the middle of the night? It's scarcely safe for a man."

"Uh, I need to get to Rocky Mountain House. There aren't any buses, and I didn't have enough money to rent a car. Besides, I'm not a very good driver." She picked her way through damp weeds back to the road. "Sorry to have bothered you, sir. You can be on your way."

It was hard to see his face in the gloom, but it looked like his dark brows drew together into a thin line. "Not if you're just going to put your thumb back out. I'm headed west into the mountains. I go right through Rocky Mountain House. I'd be glad to drop you there."

It sounded good. Too good. Megan gave herself a mental boot in the ass. Maybe if she had more information, she'd feel better about the stranger standing two feet away. "Who are you?"

"Justin McCollum." He scrabbled in a back pocket and drew out a wallet. "Look." He retrieved his flashlight, opened the wallet, and shone the light on something.

Megan stepped close enough to look. "You're a policeman?" Something tightly wound inside her relaxed in a whoosh. It didn't seem possible, but the luck that had allowed her to escape Calgary was holding.

Justin nodded. "Yes. I'm on my way to help with a fire a few miles west of Rocky Mountain House. It's out of control, and they're tapping all of us they can spare to help the firefighters."

"In that case, I accept your offer for a ride, if you're sure I won't be any trouble. Maybe I could chip in fifty cents for gas." Megan strode toward the car. He followed her and opened the passenger door.

"I wouldn't think of it." He went back around the car and settled himself behind the wheel. Once they were rolling, he glanced at her. "You never told me why you were out here in the middle of the night."

"I, uh, that is—"

"If you're just going to lie to me, don't bother." A muscle in Justin's jaw worked, and his hands tightened on the wheel. "Maybe you can listen, though."

Uh-oh.

"Sure. I can listen." She steeled herself for what felt like an imminent lecture.

"I've been a cop for a long time. Fifteen years. Looks to me like you're scared and running away from something. It's okay." He held up a hand. "You don't have to tell me a thing, but once you get to Rocky Mountain House, stay near the town."

"Because of the fire?"

"No. I don't think it will get that far. It's bound to rain soon, this late in the year. There are…abominations living in the woods. Creatures that can shift from man to beast in the blink of an eye. They make off with lone women—sometimes men too. We sent a posse out after a bunch of them about ten days back. None of them returned. Once I'm done with the fire, that's my next job. Trying to find out what happened."

Megan thought about what he'd said. "These, um, abominations. How do you know about them?"

He grimaced. "I Hunt them."

"What exactly does that mean?"

Justin shook his head. "I've said more than I should already. What's your name?"

"Um, Mary."

"Fine, Mary, but both of us know that's not really your name. Do you have any family?"

"No."

"Friends who'd take you in?"

She shook her head and then realized he was looking through the windshield. "No."

"Work acquaintances?"

Megan broke in. "I understand you're trying to find somewhere I can go. Trust me, there's nowhere. If there were, I'd have thought of it."

"What are you going to do for money? The farther you get from the cities, the harder it is to find work, and the pricier it gets to live."

"I'll look for a job. I can do housekeeping or babysitting if I have to."

"You won't find much."

Something in her rebelled. "How do you know? You don't live there. Your police card said you're from Red Deer."

"I have relatives. Say." He paused a beat. "Maybe I could help you with that job."

His offer didn't ring true. "What would you be wanting in return?"

The clouds must've parted because moonlight illuminated the car's interior. An odd look flitted across Justin's face, almost as if he'd bitten into something inexplicably bitter. "Nothing. There are no women in my life. Never have been, never will be. All of you are the same. Sex on the brain." He pulled the car to the side of the road, flicked on the dome light, and grabbed her chin between his thumb and forefinger. His blue eyes glittered dangerously.

Megan jerked her head trying to get away, but he held fast. "Now you listen up, sister. You're safe with me. I will not hurt you, and I have no interest in screwing you. Got that?"

She managed to croak out, "Yes."

He let her go as quickly as he'd seized her and guided the car back onto the road. "Now—" he went on as if their previous exchange hadn't happened "—about that job."

Holy Christ! He's crazy. He may be a cop, but he's downright nuts.

"How about this?" Megan made her voice as gentle as she could. "When you get back from the fire, you can look for me. If I haven't been able to find work, I'd be grateful for any help you could give me."

"Where will I find you?"

"Is there a ladies' boarding house in town?"

"Yes."

"Then that's where I'll be. It will be cheaper than a hotel, and they'll feed me."

"Good enough. Let me tell you more about the things you need to watch out for." He launched into an explanation of wolves, bears, coyotes, mountain cats, and birds that was so far-fetched, it made her head spin.

After listening for a while, she tapped his arm. "Justin."

"Humph."

"I appreciate all the warnings, but I didn't sleep last night. If it's all the same to you, I'd like to close my eyes until we get there."

"Of course."

His tone turned so solicitous, the fine hairs on the back of her neck twitched. He was treating her like a long lost buddy, and they barely knew one another. Something was badly wrong here, and the sooner she got out of this car, the better. Megan was sorry she'd mentioned her plan to stay at the ladies' boarding house. In such a small town, there'd only be one of them.

Ah well, I'll cross that bridge when I get to it. Maybe I'll get lucky and find a job right away. Then I won't have to deal with crazy-boy and whatever he has in mind.

~

EVEN THOUGH MEGAN didn't think she'd sleep, she must have because Justin shaking her arm brought her around. "You got a good rest, sister. We're here. I didn't want to wake you, but I've got to get rolling. I want to be at the fire line before dawn."

"Sure," she mumbled as she grappled for the door handle. "Thanks." The door finally came free, and she stepped onto an unevenly paved street. Before she could close the door, it slammed shut behind her, and the car rumbled off into the night.

Megan blinked owlishly in the moonlight at a main street that might've graced a turn of the century movie. Unlit gas lamps sat atop iron poles. The sidewalk was raised wooden slats, and the buildings looked as if they'd seen better days. They could easily be forty or fifty years old, which was probably why they had an old-timey feel. For all the construction in Calgary and Edmonton, the population boom had obviously bypassed this small community.

She walked until the buildings thinned out; it didn't take long. Where could she wait out the rest of the night? There couldn't be more than an hour or so before dawn. Though she'd napped in Justin's car, she was far from rested. A farmhouse sat off to one side of the street at the end of a long driveway. A barn snugged close to the road. Feeling like a sneak thief, she sidled toward it. If the door was open, maybe she could shelter with the animals for the night.

Megan pulled an old-fashioned latch, gratified when the rickety barn door opened with only muted creaking. Goats *baahed*. A horse snorted, blowing air through its nose. She cursed herself for not bringing a flashlight. Such a simple thing would've made her life much easier. She left the door cracked until she located a ladder leading to a loft. Returning, she latched the door and found the ladder by feel. Thank God none of its rungs were rotten. Her cloak would look a fright the next day with debris stuck in it, but Megan sank into a pile of fragrant hay.

She lay on her back and listened to the comforting sounds of animals breathing. Though she closed her eyes, sleep eluded her. Justin's words ran through her mind in an unwelcome loop and then played again. She shuddered. The man was obviously deranged. It was a stroke of fortune his brand of madness didn't extend to harming women.

She'd played dumb, but Megan knew about shifters. Nearly everybody did. Fringe elements, they mostly kept to themselves and didn't bother people, for all Justin thought they were so dangerous. She wondered if his story about losing so many of his men could possibly be true. If it was, maybe shifters were more of a threat than she'd been led to believe—at least in this remote location.

Her eyes felt hot and gritty, and her mind ran in sluggish circles. She needed at least a day to rest and regroup before she tried to find work. In her present state, no one in their right mind would hire her to so much as scrub toilets or wash clothes. She tried to firm up her plans for the following day but couldn't come up with anything solid. Daylight was seeping around the chinks in the old barn's planks when sleep finally took her.

"Woman! What are you doing in my barn?"

Megan's eyes snapped open to broad daylight. She sprang to a sit. "I-I'm sorry. It was late when I got into town. I needed a place to sleep. Everywhere was closed. I'll be on my way."

"You damn betcha you will. And right now. Round here, we don't bother with the law, we take care of things ourselves. Shoo. Shoo." The farmer, black hair flying around his face and dark eyes narrowed to wary slits, flapped one hand at her. The other curved around the stock of a shotgun.

Megan bit back a shriek and edged toward the ladder. "P-please don't shoot me. I'm trying to leave, but I need the ladder."

"Mmph. It'd serve you right if I made you jump," he grunted, but then backed down to give her access.

She hurried down the ladder's rungs and out of the barn into what had to be afternoon light. Megan shook her head in dismay. How was it possible she'd slept so long? She'd meant to be up and gone hours ago. It might've been her imagination, but the farmer's glare burned into her back as she hastened off his property.

Safe on the far side of the street—and grateful the farmer hadn't taken a shot at her—Megan glanced down at herself and groaned. Her clothes were a mass of wrinkles and peppered with straw to boot. Her hair had come loose from its pins, and hung around her in straw-studded tangles.

She put another fifty yards between herself and the irate farmer before she started picking pieces of animal feed out of her clothes, beginning with her cloak. The day wasn't too cold, so she took it off to pluck debris out of the back. It wasn't easy. Each piece of straw pulled some of the wool out of its weave. Deep in lamenting the sorry state of what had once been a fine, woolen cloak, she didn't notice the late model Ford until it rolled to a stop in front of her.

A tall woman with long, black hair and striking green eyes pushed the driver's door open, hopped from behind the wheel, and walked over to her. "Hi." She held out a hand. "I'm Alice. Feel free to tell me to piss up a rope, but if I'm any judge of things, it looks like you could use some help."

CHAPTER 3

Megan just stared at the other woman, unsure quite what to do. She looked past Alice and saw three men in the car. Suspicions flared that Alice, if that was really her name, was bait to sucker her into some dubious scheme. Megan shook her head. "I'm quite okay. It was kind of you to stop, but—"

"Bullshit," Alice said succinctly. "The boys told me to drive on past, but we women have that sixth sense thing." She winked broadly. "Anyway, my instincts were practically screaming that you needed help. You can chase me off, but I won't go easily."

"The reason I look so bad is I slept in a farmer's barn last night," Megan began but bit off the next words. No reason to tell Alice her life story. None at all. In fact, she didn't understand why she'd said anything.

A tall, lanky man with the most striking facial bone structure she'd ever seen and shoulder-length, red-gold hair got out of the passenger side of the car, followed by another man with red hair that fell halfway to his waist. The back door opened and a third man with dark hair drawn back into a braid and kind, dark eyes got out too.

All the men were impossibly good-looking. The one with hair

like an autumn sunset stepped forward and draped his arm around Alice. He held out a hand. Somehow, Megan found herself shaking it.

"I'm Jed Starnes." He beamed at her. "Alice is my wife. Bron—" he pointed at the dark-haired man "—and Terin," he gestured toward the redhead "—are my business associates and long-time friends. Brothers one and all."

"Nice to meet you," Megan stammered, remembering that once she'd had access to manners.

Jed eyed her appraisingly. "I can see where this would look a little suspicious. After all, a car with four strangers doesn't just roll up and come to a stop in front of you every day. I tried to talk Alice out of it, but—" he shrugged engagingly "—she does have a mind of her own."

Alice snorted. "Get used to it because I plan to stay that way." She wriggled from beneath Jed's embrace and stood directly in front of Megan. "What's your name?"

"Uh, Mary."

Alice frowned and bent close, drawing her dark brows together. "That's not quite right. You don't have anything to fear from us. But we can't help you if you won't tell us the truth."

Megan didn't remember asking for help. She opened her mouth to say as much but snapped it shut. It was disconcerting to realize she wanted to trust this group of people. They had an entirely different feel from Justin.

"I have a suggestion." Jed's voice held a persuasive undercurrent that was impossible to ignore. "We're on our way to visit family. I have cousins not far from here—less than ten miles. How about if you ride with us? You can tell us whatever you're comfortable sharing, and we'll drop you back in town by early evening if you'd like."

"She doesn't have anywhere to stay," Alice cut in. "If she did, she wouldn't have slept in someone's barn."

"Is that right?" Jed's blue eyes radiated concern.

Megan tried to avert her gaze, but she couldn't look away. It was as if he'd mesmerized her. "I just got into town in the middle of the night. Never had a chance to hunt for lodging."

"You told us yourself about sleeping in a barn," Alice said gently. Her smile was infectious, and Megan grinned back in spite of her reservations, which were dissipating rapidly.

Alice jabbed Jed in the side with an elbow before returning her attention to Megan. "Come on, honey. We'll have to pile a few groceries in your lap, but I'm sure we can make room."

Megan shifted from foot to foot. It wasn't as if she had anywhere else to be. Maybe fate had intervened to point her in the right direction. "Your cousins. Do you suppose they might have work for me?"

Jed quirked a brow. "They're confirmed bachelors. I'm nearly positive their house could qualify as a federal disaster area."

"Let's sort all that out as we drive." Alice strode back to the car, tugged one of its back doors open, and set to work rearranging a massive pile of groceries.

Megan smelled fresh fruit and bread. It made her mouth water, and she remembered she'd barely eaten anything the previous day.

"Come on." Alice crooked two fingers behind her back. "You're tall like me, but skinny. I think you'll fit."

Megan levered herself into the back seat and sank against a padded bench seat. It was real leather and smelled wonderful. She pulled some of the food items into her lap to make room for one of the men on the other side of the groceries.

The redhead, Terin, climbed into the back seat with her, juggling bags of food. "Help yourself if you're hungry," he said and pulled out a fresh peach.

"Where'd you get peaches this time of year?" Megan gaped at the fruit in amazement.

"We live in California. Brought lots of fruit with us. It wasn't ripe when we left home, but it is now. Want one?" He dangled a peach in front of her.

She was just biting into the succulent fruit when the front two car doors slammed shut and the car moved onto the roadway with Jed behind the wheel. Alice sat next to him, with Bron on her other side.

"You be careful." Alice waggled a finger at Jed. "Don't hurt my car."

"I'll do my best, sweetheart."

Alice, Jed, and the other two men erupted in laughter, and Megan understood it must be a standing joke. She tried to hold onto qualms about getting into this car with four strangers, but her sixth sense told her she was safe—truly safe.

"We wouldn't hurt you." Terin broke off a heel of bread and handed it to her.

"It's almost as if you can read my mind," she said around a mouthful of peach.

Terin shook his head. "I was just trying to put you at your ease. Alice is the warmest, most compassionate woman I've ever met. You're lucky she noticed you."

"I heard my name." Alice twisted around so she could look into the back seat. "Speaking of names, what's yours? And if you say Mary again, I'll be very disappointed."

"Megan."

"That's a good start." Alice nodded. "Megan what?"

"Galen."

"Want to tell us why we found you by the side of the road picking straw out of your clothes?"

Megan was shocked by how easily the words poured out of her. She even told them she had no family to turn to and that her only friends were in the cult.

"See." Alice smiled warmly. "That wasn't so hard. We'll make sure you're safe before we leave, won't we, Jed?"

He caught Megan's gaze in the rearview mirror. "Of course we will. How'd you get from Red Deer to Rocky Mountain House? Someone must have given you a ride."

Megan rolled her eyes. "I forgot about Justin. What a strange, creepy guy."

"Tell us." Terin cut off a piece of cheese and gave her more bread to put it on.

She did. The information seemed to upset the group far more than anything else she'd said. Their merry smiles faded until a pall hung over the inside of the overstuffed car. "What's wrong?" she asked at length. "Do you know him?"

"Not directly," Jed said.

"But we know his kind," Bron snapped from the front seat.

"They're trouble," Terin muttered.

Alice's heart sank. "So I'm lucky he didn't drag me off and rape me, huh?"

"He wouldn't have done that," Jed said slowly. "He was telling the truth about there not being any women in his life."

"How could you possibly know that?" Megan battled confusion. Although it wasn't possible, it seemed everyone in the car knew Justin far better than she.

"How about if we talk about something else?" Alice suggested a shade too brightly. "Like finding a job for Megan."

"We could bring her back to California," Terin said. "The cult would never find her there."

"Isn't California where Garden of Eden started?" Megan asked. She didn't want to dive from the frying pan into an even hotter fire.

"Yes, but they can't even keep track of their own members, let alone a runaway from Canada," Jed said. "Hold up, we're nearly where we're going. I need to concentrate. It's been a while since I was here last, and these forest roads all look alike to me."

∿

LES SAT in a wicker chair on the cabin's broad front porch catching the last of the day's sun. It dropped beneath the canopy of the trees long before it actually set. He scented the air and leapt to his feet. "They're almost here," he called.

Karl loped around the house, his nose twitching. "Excellent! Can't wait to meet Alice…" His voice trailed off, and he shoved his nose skyward. "I smell two women."

Les walked closer to the rutted, dirt road that led from the cabin to the main roadway. "Funny so do I. And that second one…" He inhaled deeply.

"Don't get ahead of yourself," Karl cautioned. "She smells like mate material to me too, but I'm thinking it's because we haven't been around any women for so long—other than the ones mated to our pack brothers."

Les' heart thudded in anticipation. His groin tingled, cock suddenly hard against the front of his trousers. "No. It's more than that. I get our supplies from town every month or two. I'm around women then. None of them smells like this one. I tell you, she may be who we've been waiting for."

A bittersweet pang filled his heart, and Les knew he'd given up on ever finding a mate for himself and Karl. Wolf clan shifters formed small family groups of two or three males. Once human women had vied for their attentions, but that was before Hunters had practically driven shifters like them underground.

A car engine rumbled not far off. "Well." Karl grinned. "We're about to find out. For God's sake, don't scare her off."

"Me?" Les snickered. "You're the one with a perpetual hard-on. I hear you jacking off every morning."

"Yeah, well, it's only because you do it first, and the smell of sex gets me hot."

"Ssht." Les waved a hand at Karl. "We'll alienate her before she even gets out of the car."

"Speaking of cars, wow! Wonder when Jed bought that?" Karl eyed the cream-colored Ford Cabriolet as it rolled to a stop in front of them. "Thing's so low to the ground, I'm amazed he got it back here without breaking an axle."

"Hey there, boss." Les tugged the driver's door open and held out a hand to Jed, who gripped it warmly before getting out. Terin and Bron piled out their respective doors, and the men thumped backs and shook hands.

"Alice," Jed called. "What are you waiting for, sweetheart? My cousins have heard a lot about you. They want to meet you."

"Coming."

Les watched a broad-shouldered woman as tall as himself emerge from the car. Waist-length dark hair swirled around her, and green, cat eyes slanted in an arresting, strong-boned face. He strode to her, took her hand, and pressed it to his lips. "Welcome to the pack, sister."

"So old world." She grinned at him. "Hey, Jed. You could borrow a manner or two from your kinfolk."

Karl loped over and, grabbing her hand from Les, he kissed it too. "Not to be outdone," he announced with a flourish that would've done the Count of Monte Cristo proud.

"You are such a ham." Les rolled his eyes. He turned toward the car. "Who's your friend?" he asked Alice, trying for an even tone that didn't betray his hope—or his arousal.

"Maybe I'll let Megan tell you about herself." Alice's green eyes danced mischievously. "She's feeling a little shy. All you men can feel a bit overwhelming. She said something about letting you get your hellos out of the way."

"Can I help with making her more comfortable?" Les asked, and then realized Karl was already over at the car bending so he could peer inside. "Never mind." He raced to Karl's side and almost stopped breathing. The woman sitting in the back seat with food piled around her was exquisite. Blonde hair hung to her waist. A pair of inquisitive sky-blue eyes peered up at him. High cheekbones, a well-formed chin, and full lips that looked imminently kissable hit Les with all the subtlety of a runaway freight.

"She's our mate!" Karl cried in their telepathic speech.

"Yes, but she has to agree. Remember the rules. We can't use magic, and we need to take this slow," Les cautioned.

He was having a hell of a time. He didn't want to take anything slow. What he wanted was to sweep Megan into his arms and crush her against him, right before he covered those lush lips with his own. Scenes of sharing her long, lean body with Karl bombarded him until he couldn't think.

"Hi." Her gaze moved from him to Karl and back. "I was just waiting until everyone was done catching up." She shrugged self-consciously. "I wouldn't want to horn in on your family time."

"Welcome." Karl extended a hand. "Do you need help getting out?" He pulled the car door open wider.

Les kicked himself for not asking first.

"No, silly. I'm not crippled." Megan moved the groceries in her lap to the car's seat, swung her legs out, and stood. She wore a long, black cloak that obscured whatever she had under it. Still, Les saw the swell of high, firm breasts and a rounded ass. "Here." She turned back to the car. "Let me help get all this food inside."

"We can all do that." Alice trotted up from somewhere.

Les didn't feel capable of anything except staring at Megan. He was surprised to find himself heading for the cabin with a full load of groceries and wondered who'd heaped them into his arms.

The next half hour passed in a blur. Megan had rubbed up against him so many times as they'd passed one another with armloads of foodstuffs that his groin ached, and his mind felt like mush.

She'd been aroused too. He'd smelled it. With her heat had come blushes and excuses and way too many instances of, "I'm sorry," and "excuse me," for his taste. Karl had drawn her aside at one point and tried to wrap his arms around her, but she'd slithered away.

"That's all of it," Jed said, hooking his arms through Les and Karl's. "Alice escorted Megan outside for a little, um, chat. We're going to stay in here and come up with something passable for supper while the ladies talk."

"Shit! I didn't realize she'd left." Karl tugged against Jed's hold. "Let go of me. Les and I have to talk to her."

Bron stepped close and shook his head. "Alice is really good at this. She can explain things better than you can. Especially the shape you two are in." He shot a meaningful glance at the belled-out crotches of their pants.

"Yes, Alice got a whole lot more of our magic than I expected she would," Jed cut in. "She's found mates for three family groups in just the short time she's been with us. Damn if I know how she sniffs the women out, but it's why she stopped when she saw Megan today."

Les pulled free of Jed and raked his hands through his hair. "How long will we have to wait?"

"We don't know," Terin said. "Each time Alice has done this, it's been different. Basically, she's explaining our mating ritual. If Megan agrees—"

"What do you mean if?" Karl shouted. "She has to."

"No," Les said slowly. "She doesn't. If she decides being mated to us is too much for her, we'll erase her memory, and Jed can take her back where he found her." Anxiety sat like a lead weight in his gut. Les hated feeling helpless. He also didn't like trusting something this important to another person.

A hand settled on his shoulder. Les turned to see Jed's blue eyes focused on him. "I almost lost Alice," he said. "I was so anxious to get her into my bed, I didn't tell her about Bron and Terin. When she found out, she was angry. More than angry, furious. We were in the mountains and she ran from me. A mountain lion attacked her. I switched to my wolf form and took on the cat, but it very nearly killed me. Would have if I hadn't had Bron, our most talented healer, by my side."

"What a mess that was," Terin muttered. "It took all of us, including Alice, to save Jed."

"Holy shit!" Les speared Jed with troubled eyes. "How come we never heard about that?"

"What?" Jed grunted. "I'm supposed to broadcast my stupid mistakes to the whole clan? I don't think so. The only reason I told you was to underscore how precarious things are until Megan decides you two are worth everything she'll have to give up to join her life to yours."

Karl brought a fist down on one of the counters. "I want to crawl out of my skin, and my wolf's been damn nigh uncontrollable since we scented Megan." His tortured dark gaze sought Jed's. "At least you had a chance to botch things up on your own."

Jed grimaced. "Never fear, you'll have plenty of opportunity to botch things. Even if she's agreeable to the concept of being mated to shifters, the lady will want to get to know the two of you a little before she binds herself to you forever."

"In the meantime—" Bron shouldered his way to the woodstove "—let's do our part and at least make a good faith effort to get a meal together for the women."

"Good idea," Terin seconded. "They may be out there for quite some time."

Les groaned. Waiting felt impossible. He stomped to one of the piles of food littering the kitchen counters. "Meat," he grumbled. "We need meat to get through this."

"We'll probably need more than a little." Jed pursed his mouth. "Aren't the rest of the local clan showing up soon?"

"I called them," Les said. "You told me you were going to be here for a few days, so we set up a gathering for night after next. Karl and I thought it would be good to give you some breathing room after such a long drive."

"Excellent. We do need to talk with them." Bron drummed his fingers on the table. "This will save us a bunch of time running everybody down."

CHAPTER 4

egan had headed back outside for another load of food and supplies only to find the car empty. Thank God. If ever she needed a break to clear her head, it was now. She leaned her overheated forehead on one of the car's windows, reveling in its cool, smooth surface. If she'd thought Jed, Bron, and Terin handsome, it was only because she hadn't met Les or Karl yet. What gorgeous men! Both were tall and lean with broad, well-muscled shoulders and slender hips. She'd gotten such a huge sexual jolt from being in the same room with them, Megan found herself "accidentally" brushing up against one or the other during their multiple trips back and forth to the car.

She pushed her hair away from her face and continued to let the car's window cool her. It had taken all her self-control not to simply drag Les or Karl—or better yet, both of them—behind the cabin and strip off her clothes. Never mind that she'd never considered such an action before in her life. A fresh wave of heat burned its way up her neck, suffusing her face. Two men. What the hell was she thinking?

I'm thinking about getting laid. That's what. Giving up my virginity. Christ! I'm twenty-five years old. What on earth am I holding out for?

While Karl had long, dark, shiny hair that begged her to run her fingers through it, Les' was tawny-colored. He had his pulled back in a braid, but it, too, begged to be finger-combed. And his eyes were the most incredible shade of moss green, deep like shaded mountain pools she'd seen in picture books at the library. Karl's eyes were so dark a woman could lose her soul in them. Megan blew out a breath. It frosted against the car window. She'd thought a break away from Les and Karl might clear her mind, but it was just as muddled as when she'd come outside a few minutes before.

Her nipples were hard as stones, her breasts heavy with need, and that special, wild place between her legs throbbed with heat. Though technically still a virgin, she'd done plenty of necking and petting with the men at cult gatherings. They'd brought one another to orgasm many times through everything but actual fucking. No stranger to sexual need, she'd never been anywhere near as hot as she was right this minute.

Maybe if I make myself come...

She straightened and gazed around the clearing. It wouldn't take but a few moments to slip into the thickly wooded area beyond the cabin, take care of herself, and—

"There you are." Alice's cheery voice rang out. In moments the other woman stood beside her. "You look as if you could stand a bit of a walk and some conversation." Megan opened her mouth, but Alice shushed her with a look. "I know exactly how you feel. It's the same thing that happened to me when I first ran across Jed."

Interest kindled. Megan exhaled and dragged her attention away from her crotch. "I have a feeling you're going to tell me about it."

"That I am. Come on." Alice held out a hand. Megan hesitated and then grasped it. Something calming seemed to emanate from Alice. Megan relaxed into the sensation of being understood and taken care of.

"I was in the Sierra Nevada Mountains climbing with a friend," Alice began. "He ran off and left me—"

"What?" Megan stopped walking. "But that's terrible. He should be shot."

"It was okay." Alice got them moving again in a large circle just inside the tree line around the house. "I found my way down. Anyway, I was almost to the trail when Jed sort of melted out of the shadows. He talked me into going into Lon Chaney's cabin with him."

"The movie star?"

Alice tossed her head back and laughed. "The same. Jed knows him—Chaney Junior, that is. They work together at the movie studio, but that's not the important part. What was most significant for me—and now for you—was how I felt around Jed. I wanted him in ways I'd never wanted a man before, and he was so irresistible, I begged him to bed me once we'd talked about a lot of things."

Megan cocked her head to one side and glanced sidelong at Alice. "What kind of things?"

"I'm getting to that." Alice came to a halt, stepped in front of Megan, and placed hands on her shoulders. "Look at me, so you'll know I'm telling you the truth."

Megan's heart crashed against her chest. In the deepest recesses of her being, she intuited that Alice's next words would change her life forever.

"Yes," Alice said softly, "they will."

"You can read my mind?"

Alice nodded. "To some extent. There's no easy way to say this next part, Megan, so I'll just spit it out. All these men are wolf shifters. Jed, Bron, and Terin are my mates." Alice leveled her gaze at Megan. "Karl and Les would like to be yours."

The world spun, crazy and out of control. Spots danced in front of Megan's eyes, and she swayed on her feet. "I don't understand why I'm not screaming like a banshee and running to get away from you," she muttered.

"Because I'm using magic to help you stay in one place long enough to hear me out. Now that I've told you, though, you do have a choice. If you want to hear more, great, but if you want me to drive you back to Rocky Mountain House, I can do that too. Jed and the rest of them have a way of erasing your memories of ever meeting us."

Megan thought about Les and Karl and how attracted she was to them. "Is that why the men feel so irresistible?"

Alice nodded. "It's the mate bond. Would you like to hear about it?" She lifted her hands from Megan's shoulders and dropped her arms to her sides. "You need to make this choice on your own, not because I coerced you with shifter magic. Jed can turn it on and off. I'm not quite that adept yet, so I have to stop touching you."

Megan took a step back and then another. A voice inside her head screamed at her to walk away from what was surely madness, but another reminded her how little she had in her life. There was nothing to go back to, not really. She bit her lower lip. "That man who drove me to Rocky Mountain House. He said he Hunts shifters. That must have been why you all got so quiet when I told you about him."

Alice nodded. "It's also why he wouldn't have harmed you. Hunters take vows of chastity and obedience to their order. My friend—" She shook her head angrily. "Don't know why I keep calling Brent a friend. He's who left me in the mountains. Anyway, he was a Hunter, and he'd scented Jed and the boys. It's why he took off after them and left me to figure things out on my own."

"He'd have left you to die to go after shifters?"

"Yes. They put their vows before everything else. Otherwise, they'd never be able to stay celibate."

Megan started walking again. Alice paced her to one side.

"How much more can you tell me before I have to make a decision?"

"I can tell you everything you want to know—or most of it, anyway—but if you make love with Les and Karl, you'll be bound to them for the rest of your life. It's not that you wouldn't be able to leave, but no other man will ever appeal to you, and you'll pine for your mates for the rest of your days."

Megan broke into wry laughter. "Hell, I can see myself doing that now, and neither of them has laid a hand on me."

"Let me tell you about the mate bond."

Nodding slowly, Megan turned to face Alice. "Okay. I think I'd like to hear about it. You certainly seem happy."

A beatific smile split Alice's high-cheekboned face. "Happy doesn't even come close. I never imagined the joy those three men could bring to my life. I don't lack for a thing. They love me, take care of me, and let me be who I am." She spread her arms wide. "I'm an engineer. It was important to me to keep working, so I did. Jed has oodles of money. So do Bron and Terin, but they want me to do what fulfills me." Alice rolled her eyes. "I'm getting off track. The mate bond has become rarer because shifters have had to go into hiding these past couple hundred years. They need time in their animal forms to spur the urge to bond—and human women who will want them."

"Aren't there any shifter women?"

"Yes and no. All shifters are born male. When we mate with them, we receive some of their shifter magic through semen and the mate bond. Any sons we bear will be shifters. Daughters will be like us and have some shifter magic."

"How do I know Les and Karl are supposed to be my mates?"

Alice quirked a brow. "I think you could answer that one yourself. I watched you in there." She hooked a thumb toward the cabin. "You had a hard time not brushing up against the guys. And they were having a hell of a time not just crushing you to them. The mate bond is hard to explain, but it connects me to my mates. It's so compelling, I can't help but love them and they me."

"And you felt like that about Jed from the minute you saw him?"

"You bet I did. And I was damned if I understood why I wanted him so much I was willing to break every social convention in the book to get his cock inside me." She lowered her voice. "Within an hour of meeting him, he got me so hot I ended up masturbating myself in front of him. Jesus! Was I ever mortified. I was afraid I was turning into a nymphomaniac."

The heat she'd denied earlier rushed in with a vengeance. Megan squirmed as she rubbed her damp thighs together.

"I know exactly how you're feeling." Alice repeated her earlier words. "Like you'll die if you don't come. It's the mate bond. Nothing else has that effect. How do you think Les and Karl are feeling? They're probably tearing their hair out inside that cabin." She snorted. "Bet Jed and the boys have had to hog-tie them to keep them from barreling out here."

The image was humorous, but Megan didn't let herself laugh. "I need time to assimilate all this."

"Of course you do." Alice patted her arm. "Tell you what. I'm going to sit on the steps. You go ahead and pace up and down the yard, or sit in the car, or do whatever you need to come to terms with what must feel impossible. I can't let you out of my sight because if you decide this life isn't for you, Jed will make sure you don't remember any of us. It's not that we don't trust you, but someone like Justin can read your mind too, and it's not safe if you hold images of us in your thoughts."

"I understand." Megan pressed her tongue against her teeth. "Probably better that way because Les and Karl would haunt me, and I'd always wonder if I'd made a big mistake."

"Well," Alice said pragmatically, "you're still here. If you think you'd like to explore the possibilities further, your next step will be to get to know Karl and Les a little better. You'll love them because of the mate bond, but you need to like them as people too."

Megan nodded. She put distance between herself and Alice in the darkening yard and paced in a tight circle. Someone had lit lanterns inside the cabin. A merry, golden light spilled through the windows, illuminating sections of the clearing. The smell of roasting meat wafted out. Megan clasped her hands behind her back and thought long and deep. She already felt something bright and shining anchoring her to Les and Karl. It was the most compelling sensation she'd ever experienced. It was sexual, but so much more than that too.

What happens to my life? This isn't the sort of arrangement I could actually tell people about. I'd be a social pariah.

Yeah, right. Like I'm not already.

Megan clicked off pros and cons in her mind. She was on the run from the only life she'd made for herself. It wasn't as if she had a plethora of options waiting. No, she'd planned to bury herself in the Canadian hinterlands. Not much of a life, but better than being hunted down by the Garden of Edeners and used as an example and a sacrifice. Even if she only lost a few fingers, being trapped into remaining with the cult until she died was no sort of existence at all.

She squared her shoulders, inhaled deeply, blew out the breath, and then did it again before marching resolutely to where Alice sat on the cabin's steps. "I want to spend time getting to know Les and Karl."

Alice leapt to her feet and swept Megan into a hug about the same time whoops sounded from inside the cabin. Megan hugged Alice back. "They were listening to us the whole time?"

Alice let go of her and shrugged. "Well, their hearing isn't quite as sharp in their human form, but I don't think they had to work very hard to eavesdrop."

The cabin door banged open. All five men crowded out. Jed

took Alice by the arm. "We're going back to town tonight to get some rooms."

"Excellent idea," Alice seconded. "It will give them privacy."

"Surely you'll stay for supper," Megan protested. "I've smelled it cooking for a while now."

"Nah." Bron trotted to the car. "Be sure to save some food, though. We'll be back tomorrow around noon."

"Don't hurry," Les called after his retreating form.

"Besides, this will give us privacy too," Jed noted with a wink at Alice.

"Ooooh, now I really like the sound of that." She leaned against him and laid her head on his shoulder.

In a sudden burst of concern over what she'd gotten herself into, Megan made a grab for Alice's arm just as the other woman turned toward the car. "Promise me you'll come back just in case, well in case things don't um…"

Alice bent close and whispered in her ear. "You have my word. But, sweetie, I'm betting you'll be sorry when you hear us pull into the drive tomorrow because it'll mean you have to get out of bed."

LES WATCHED the Ford make a three point turn and get headed back to the main road. He felt suddenly nervous. So much was riding on this, neither he nor Karl could afford to make any mistakes. He cleared his throat. "Karl and I want to thank you," he began.

"We certainly do," Karl cut in.

"For what? I haven't done anything yet."

"For giving us a chance," Les said. "I know this is something really different from what you must be used to."

"In some ways but not all." Megan wrapped her arms around her slender form.

"Come inside." Karl was solicitousness itself. "There's a fire going."

"Yes," Les chimed in. "We have a meal underway."

"It's nearly done," Karl added.

"Even better." Les grinned. "We'll eat and you can ask us anything you want."

Megan laughed. "Do the two of you always finish each other's sentences?"

Les took her arm and led her up the steps and into the cabin that he hoped would become their home. "'Fraid so. It's because we've lived together for so long."

"Yeah," Karl said as he pulled the door shut behind them. "We have the same problem when we're wolves. He tries to out-howl me. Come and sit." He patted an empty place at a scarred oak table in the middle of the kitchen side of the cabin.

"Please sit. We'll serve you." Les smiled. He felt like a besotted fool, but looking at Megan made his heart light and his head giddy.

"Bosh." Megan headed for the stove. "I'm used to cooking. I can take over from here."

"Not a chance." Karl steered her back toward the table and pulled out a chair. "Let us spoil you a little. We've dreamed of having a mate to cherish and care for."

"Really?" Megan's voice came out as a squeak as she sat down.

"Really." Les dished up the soup Karl had made and carried it to the table. Even though he was used to Karl's cooking, it smelled wonderful, no doubt due to the infusion of ingredients from Jed. "We've had a whole lot of years to imagine what it would be like if we had a mate."

"But you can't be much past thirty-five." Megan reached for the soup tureen and set it next to waiting bowls.

Les and Karl exchanged glances. Karl put a plate of sliced bread on the table, and Les returned to the kitchen to get a platter of succulent-looking meat and an open bottle of wine. "Alice didn't actually tell you everything," Les said. "Shifters live long lives."

Her eyes narrowed. "How long?"

Here we go.

Les sucked in a breath. Lying at this point wasn't permitted. The prospective mate needed to know everything. "I'm close to six hundred."

"And I've got fifty years on him," Karl said. "But you'll live longer too. Not quite as long as we do, but the mate bond will lengthen your life."

"Really?" Megan had a stunned look on her face. "Guess Alice only hit the high points. Are Jed and Bron and Terin that old too?"

Les let his fisted hands relax by his sides. This was going better than he'd hoped. At least she hadn't jumped up and run out of the cabin. "Jed's a few hundred years older than Karl and I. I'm not sure about Terin or Bron."

"Could I have some of that wine?" Megan pointed, still looking shell-shocked.

Karl ran into Les when they both made a dive for the bottle. "Sorry." Les smiled sheepishly and filled the glass in front of her with claret-colored liquid. "We're so anxious to make a good impression, we're acting like a couple of buffoons."

She lifted her glass. Megan's gaze traveled from him to Karl and back. "Aren't the two of you going to sit?"

Les scrambled into his seat. So did Karl. The last thing Les felt like doing was eating, but wine wasn't a bad idea. Maybe it would settle the hard-on he'd had ever since Megan drove into their yard.

"Before you take a drink," Megan said, "I'd like to propose a toast."

Les winced. He or Karl should've done that. The first meal with a prospective mate was nothing shy of a momentous occasion. "Of course." He lifted his glass and looked expectantly at her.

"Nothing too serious." She still looked nervous, but managed a smile. "Here's to getting to know one another."

They clinked glasses and drank. Les gazed around the table that could accommodate half a dozen and imagined finally filling their home with children. He reined his thoughts in. "Do you have everything you need?" he asked Megan.

"I'm not sure." Her blue eyes twinkled at him and Karl. "But it's starting to look that way."

Karl ladled the meat and vegetable soup he'd made into bowls. "None of us are probably very hungry," he said, "but how about if you tell us about you, and then we can do the same."

"My story won't take very long." Megan spooned soup into her mouth. "I lost my entire family in the flu epidemic of 1918. Got sent to an orphanage from there. I finished school, went to work, and then a couple of years ago I got mixed up with a cult, which is why I have some familiarity with, er, different lifestyles…"

CHAPTER 5

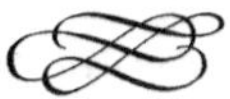

egan didn't know how long they talked, but the food left on the table had long since grown cold when conversation finally thinned. She gazed fondly at the men sitting near her. In the hours they'd shared food and drink, her heart had warmed to both of them. Les and Karl were good men. Even more, they were kind and compassionate but willing to stand and fight for their beliefs and the freedom of their kind.

Born in the fourteen hundreds, they'd become fast friends in the Black Forest in Germany where they'd roamed as wolves and young men. Both were descended from Hohenzollern bloodlines, and their kin had originally ruled Prussia, Germany, and Romania. Somewhere around the early eighteen hundreds, the Catholic Swabian branch and the Protestant Franconian branch of the Hohenzollern family finally agreed on one thing: shifters were demon spawn. At that point, Les and Karl set sail for the new world, along with many other shifters.

They'd had one mate, Breta, but she died in childbirth in 1699 and the babe along with her. Apparently a major vessel in her heart ruptured while she was in labor, and all the shifter magic in the world couldn't save her. Both men were devastated and too dispirited to even consider mating again anytime soon. Tears glistened in Karl's eyes when he told her about their first mate. Though she'd been gone for over two hundred years, it was clear he still missed her. And reproached himself for her death.

"You've been quiet for a while." Karl poured the last of a second bottle of wine into her glass.

"I was thinking about Breta." Megan looked into Karl's dark, hypnotic eyes and thought she could see his pain. "I'm so sorry for your loss, but you really shouldn't blame yourself. These things happen even today with all the modern medical interventions we have."

"I've told him that for a long time," Les said quietly.

Karl nodded. "We've mourned Breta long enough. She wouldn't have wanted us to be alone for a year, let alone two hundred."

"It's not that we were averse to finding a new mate," Les said.

"But once we started looking," Karl cut in, "we never found anyone who clicked with our mate bond."

"Are eligible women that rare then?" She looked from one man to the other.

"Much more than they used to be," Karl replied. "Having to hide out from Hunters hasn't helped us much. I'm sure they hope we'll all die out, and then they will have done their job for God and country." His words dripped bitterness. He shook his head. "Sorry, I hate those bastards, and sometimes it bleeds out of me, but they don't have any place here in this room tonight with us."

"No," Les concurred. "They don't." He got up, closed the distance between himself and Megan, and knelt by her chair. "You've heard all about Karl and me. You see the life we lead. It's not fancy, especially compared with the castles and servants we had in the old world, but we have everything we need—except you. If you found it too isolating out here and living in town was important, we'd figure something out. Maybe have two houses. Though we live simply, money's not a problem."

Karl knelt by her other side and took one of her hands. His dark eyes grew serious. "Yes, there's not much more talking to be done. Les always tells me I'm too forward, but will you have us, Megan?"

"We'd love and cherish you," Les murmured.

"You'd never want for a thing," Karl said.

Megan looked from one set of eyes to the other. Both men's hearts were in their faces. She believed them. More, she wanted them as passionately as they wanted her. She twined a hand in Les' tawny hair and squeezed Karl's hand. "Yes," she murmured, and then said it more clearly. "Yes, I accept the mate bond. Right now I'm feeling like the luckiest woman alive."

"We'll make sure that never changes." Karl lifted her hand to his lips. Les snatched her other hand from his hair and did the same.

Heat suffused her face, and she figured she was blushing furiously. "I suppose I ought to tell you I'm still a virgin."

Les stopped kissing the back of her hand. "We knew that, darling. It doesn't matter. We're delighted that we'll be your first lovers."

She cocked her head to one side. What the men were doing to her hands was incredibly erotic. "How did you know? Is it a scent thing?"

Karl lifted his head and murmured, "Um-hum," before exchanging glances with Les. "Where?"

Les brushed his thumb over her lips and got to his feet. "We'll need a bigger bed. For now, maybe we could put your mattress on the floor next to mine."

Karl laid his cheek next to Megan's and planted a string of nibbling kisses down her ear.

"Hey there, bud." Les hooked an arm beneath Karl's. "We'll have lots of time for that. Help me move the mattress."

"Oh, sure. Right." Karl's breath came fast.

Megan sensed his arousal and it fueled hers. "I'll get the table cleared while the two of you are—"

"Not on your life, darling," Les said as he and Karl headed for a curtained alcove toward the rear of the cabin.

"We'll take care of everything. You just sit," Karl seconded.

"Now that's plain silly. You're treating me as if I were an invalid." Megan rose and swept the cabin with her gaze. "I'll heat water in the big kettle on the woodstove. That way we can all clean up a bit before, well..." Megan's face warmed still more, right along with the rest of her. The temperature in the small space felt as if it had just risen twenty degrees. She fanned herself with both hands.

"Grand idea." Les grabbed one end of a mattress. He and Karl moved it toward a closed door that presumably led to the bedroom.

Grateful to have something to do—and glad it didn't require much thought because she was so aroused her brain felt like yesterday's oatmeal—Megan walked to the woodstove, opened the firebox door, and fed some chunks of wood through it. Her swollen labia pressed against one another. Scenes of Les and Karl naked danced before her eyes. She couldn't wait to run her hands over their hard-muscled bodies and kiss and taste them.

She'd just pumped one last container of water at the sink and carried it to the kettle when the men emerged from the bedroom. Megan dipped a hand into the kettle. "Not quite yet," she said, "but soon."

"We can hurry that along." Les hastened to her side, placed fingers in the kettle, and hummed a few notes. "There. Perfect bathing temperature."

She quirked a brow. "Magic?"

He grinned. "What else? This is a magical household, and tonight is a magical night. We've waited a long time for you."

"Well, I'm just glad some other gal didn't ace me out because I like it here." She grinned back. "Help me understand about the water. If you did something and it's hot enough now, won't the fire make it too hot to use soon?"

"No." Karl started pulling the few pins left in her hair out. Blonde strands settled around her body, and she brushed them away from her face. "Shifter magic is good for lots of things. Keeping water at a particular temperature is one of the lesser spells."

"You said I'd get some of your magic. Will I be able to—?"

Les caressed the side of her face. "It's different for every mate. We won't know until after the mating ritual is complete."

"You tell us how you'd like to do this," Karl said. "Les and I talked it over while we made up the bed and decided you need to set the pace."

She inhaled a little, hiccupy breath. "If we're going to bathe, we have to get out of these clothes." Her blush deepened and she rolled her eyes. "Christ! I sound brain-damaged. And like a nervous bride."

"No, you don't." Les' tone was soothing. "You're still a maid, and you're anxious about what's going to happen. It's understandable. Would you like us to help you undress? We can do as much or as little as you'd like, including giving you a spot of privacy to bathe."

A streak of lechery smote her. When she met his gaze, she was certain she had a wanton gleam in her eyes. "How about if I get to watch you first? Or—" she squared her shoulders and faced both men "—how about if I undress you?"

Where did I learn to be so bold?

Megan glanced down. Her tongue felt thick and stupid when she said, "I, uh, I'm sorry. I have no idea where that came from."

"You have nothing to apologize for." Karl's rich laughter filled the cabin. "Come here, darling. You can start with me. It would be an honor for you to undress me."

"Come on." Les took her hand and led her the few steps to Karl.

Megan's hands shook as she raised them and began on the buttons of Karl's shirt. He'd taken off his sweater during dinner. She pushed the flannel material off his shoulders and gasped when his perfectly formed torso came into view. A dusting of black hair coated the bronze skin of an otherwise smooth chest. Slabs of muscle descended into the waistband of his trousers. The front was tented by an obvious erection.

Megan's mouth was dry, and her breath came in little, panting gasps. All the moisture in her body had headed south. Her clit and labia were puffy and aching, and she was so hot she thought she might come with no additional stimulation at all. She reached for the fastenings of his trousers when a low, keening moan sounded. It took a moment for her to realize the noise had come from her. Les reached around her from behind. He laid a hand over one of her breasts and dropped the other to the vee between her legs. Megan pressed into him.

"That's right, sweetheart." Les' voice was hoarse with need. "Unbutton him and I'll just rub you a little. We have all night, and we'll all think better after we've come a time or two."

Megan undid Karl's trousers. His cock sprang into her hands. It was hot, hard, and so thick she needed both hands to span it. Karl groaned and thrust himself into her grip. Les rubbed her clit through her skirts. In moments, Megan felt an orgasm spool deep in her belly. She milked Karl's cock harder and harder as a climax ripped through her.

A hand settled over hers, and she realized Karl was helping her, showing her what he needed. A few more strokes and he shrieked some words in German as hot semen spattered her hands. When his cock stopped jumping and spurting, she tilted her head and he kissed her, long and slow. His tongue slid into her mouth, and she welcomed the taste and feel of him.

Les kept on rubbing her nipple and clit. His mouth worked its way up her neck. She felt his erection press against her buttocks. Karl raised his lips from hers.

"Turn around, darling," he urged. "Les needs you too."

Megan turned in Les' arms and started on his shirt. "Never mind that part," Les murmured and moved her hands to his pants. She cupped the outline of his cock through them and then worked the button and zipper loose.

She could feel him but not see him. His cock felt even thicker than Karl's. Megan sank to her knees so she could take a look. Proud and hard, Les' penis rose from a mat of tawny hair. It was a little shorter than Karl's, but indeed, thicker. Megan bent toward him and licked experimentally at the smooth glans. His cock twitched in her fingers. He laid a hand on either side of her head and guided her to him. She took his shaft into her mouth, thrilled by the way it stretched her.

Karl sat next to her and twirled her nipples before sinking one hand between her legs. He worked his way beneath her skirts, and the skin-to-skin contact nearly undid her. Megan sucked harder. Les' cock got even bigger and firmer in her mouth. Riding on instinct, she reached around him, grasped his ass, and pulled him as close as she could. Her teeth grazed the sides of his dick. With an inchoate moan, he drove himself harder and faster into her mouth.

Megan knew what came next. She'd never actually swallowed come, but she'd always wanted to. When he tried to pull away, she gripped his buttocks and held fast. His cock geysered into her mouth. Feeling it jump and spurt gave her the most amazing feeling of power, plus it made her hotter than hell.

Karl still worked her with his knowing fingers. As soon as Les was done coming, Karl pushed her gently backward onto the floor, pulled her skirts and panties out of the way, and replaced his fingers with his mouth. The sensation of him sucking her sensitive nub was so unexpected and intense, she shrieked her delight as another climax roared through her.

Once her spasms subsided, Karl raised his head. "Think two

will hold you so we can get through that bath before all the water evaporates?"

Megan giggled. Having two men all to herself might be much better than anything she'd ever dreamed about. Alice had three. For a moment, she wondered how that worked but then batted it aside. It didn't matter what Alice had. She didn't want Jed or Terin or Bron. She was right where she belonged, with her mates, Les and Karl.

"Yes." Megan struggled to sit and found herself boosted to her feet by four helping hands. "Two orgasms will do it, but only for now, mind you."

"Whew." A brilliant smile lit Les' Greek god features. "Because we've just been getting warmed up."

Karl patted his still half-hard cock. "There's a lot more where this came from. Hey! You still have most of your clothes on."

"Yeah." Les unwrapped the cloak she'd never removed. "How'd that happen?"

"It happened," she said, trying to mimic a patronizing tone of voice and failing utterly, "because the two of you let me undress you first and we got...sidetracked."

Karl snorted. "Sidetracked, eh?"

"We'll show you sidetracked." Les pulled her dark blue sweater over her head and unhooked her plain, white bra.

Karl whistled. "Beautiful," he breathed. "Just beautiful. Gorgeous tits."

"I agree. We're very lucky men." Les cupped her breasts in his hands and bent to kiss one, but only for a moment. "Most blondes have washed out nipples, but yours are the color of ripe straw-berries."

"You can kiss them some more." She made a grab for him, but he went to work on the buttons holding her navy blue wool skirt in place.

"No more kisses for the moment," Karl said. "We heated that

water and by God, we're going to use it. Maybe now I'll be able to get Les to clean up more often."

"Speak for yourself." Les tugged and her skirt slithered to the floor. Megan gave a little shove, and her soaked cotton panties followed it.

She spread her arms wide. "All ready." She started for the steaming kettle.

"Hold it right there." Les hurried in front of her, snagged a towel from a drawer, and dipped it into the hot water. He wrung it out and turned so he could run it down her body. The warm terrycloth felt wonderful. Megan inhaled deeply and closed her eyes. She felt two cloths stroking her. When she opened her eyes, both men were washing her.

"What do you think about soap?" Les asked.

"Too hard to rinse without a proper washtub," Karl answered.

"One of many things we'll need to get," Les murmured.

"How have you been bathing?" Megan felt confused.

Les snorted. "We're tough guys. We have a cold water shower hooked up out back."

"I'll say you're tough." Megan turned to give them better access to her backside. "You do that even in the winter?"

"Not so much." A corner of Karl's mouth turned downward. "Hence my comment about taking advantage of your presence to enhance our grooming efforts."

"So, what did you do before?" she persisted.

"In the winter, we spend a lot of time as wolves," Les said. "If our pelts felt dirty, we'd scratch a hole in an icy stream and wash. Or just roll in the snow."

Megan stepped away from the men, bent over the kettle, and sluiced water over her hands and face. She straightened, grabbed a towel, and dried herself before turning to face them. Karl was naked; Les still had his shirt on. She went to him and unbuttoned his shirt, pushing it off his shoulders. He was more heavily muscled than Karl, with more golden skin tones. His skin was smooth but for a very few curly hairs around his copper-colored nipples.

"Good thing you had us take our shoes off before we sat down to eat," she said. "It would have been awkward getting your trousers over them."

"We've always done that," Karl said.

Les nodded. "Yes, back in the old country, we removed our shoes in the castle mudroom and replaced them with house slippers. Rather, servants did that for us. It helped keep the dirt they had to clean to a manageable level, I suppose."

"Aren't either of you going to at least rinse off?" Megan placed her hands on her hips and looked meaningfully at the hot water.

"You heard the lady." Karl headed for the kettle. He still had the cloth he'd used to wash her, and he dipped it back into the water to wash himself. Les followed suit. It wasn't the most bang-up cleaning job, but it would do.

"Ready to come to bed?" Les tossed his washrag into the kitchen sink and smiled at her.

"I thought you'd never ask." Megan held out both hands. Les grasped one and Karl the other. Bodies bumping against each other, they laughingly made their way through a doorway much too narrow to accommodate three.

"Oh my." Megan's hand flew to her mouth. "It's lovely." The men had laid an inviting-looking bed, piled high with colorful comforters and pillows, and set candles to burn in the corners of the room. Scented with mint and jasmine, they made the bedroom smell heavenly.

"If we'd have had flower petals, we'd have scattered them." Les smiled softly.

"And gold and jewels." Karl grinned too. "You'll have to give us a few days to treat you like the queen you are—our queen."

Megan's throat thickened with emotion. "Aw, guys." She blinked back tears. "Those things aren't important. We already have what's most important. Each other." Letting go of their hands, Megan covered the few steps to the bed and laid down. The men converged, one on either side, and held her between them.

She snuggled between two wonderfully masculine bodies, reveling in the heady scent they produced that was sex incarnate. Les and Karl drew closer, whispering how much they adored her.

She sat up between them and laid a hand on each man's shoulder. "The two of you are wonderfully romantic, but could we please get cracking on divesting me of my virginity and getting some of that shifter magic cooking so I can heat water too? We have the rest of our lives for you to tell me how wonderful I am."

"You heard the lady," Les said.

"That I did." Karl pulled her back down between them and kissed her cheek. "Your wish is our command."

A thrill ran up her spine. Two men, all for her. Life couldn't possibly get any sweeter than this.

CHAPTER 6

$\mathcal{L}$es ran kisses down Megan's neck and settled in the hollow of her collarbones to lick the sweetness from her skin. She tasted incredible. He'd loved how responsive she was to his and Karl's caresses. It was as if she'd been born to have two lovers. He moved lower and captured a nipple. It was already pebble-hard, but it puckered still more as he tongued it.

"Which one of us first?" Karl's voice sounded in his mind.

Les sent a prayer to Gaia for the gift she'd given shifters. There were no jealousies in their family packs. Everyone gave a hundred ten percent, and no one ever kept score. Les lifted his mouth from Megan's breast. Karl still lay next to her, mouth glued to hers as they kissed deeply. He felt the other man's arousal as acutely as his own. Despite his earlier climax, his cock was so hard it ached. Les knew it was the mate bond driving them. The urge to couple was so strong, it made shifters physically ill if they tried to deny it.

"You can take her," Les replied, *"but let me get her ready so it doesn't hurt so much."*

"Hurry. I'm afraid I'll come before I even get inside."

Les returned to sucking Megan's nipples, moving from one to the other while he slid a hand between her legs. He smiled to himself. She was more than aroused. Her passion-slick nub thrummed beneath his questing fingers. If he did things right, he wanted to get her so hot she was ready to climax. Extreme arousal would help her push through the pain of being deflowered. Or maybe he could take care of that part with his fingers.

Les trailed kisses down her stomach and settled between her legs. She came so easily, he'd have to be careful to keep her hovering on the edge. He licked her clit, first one side, then the other, and then tried a lazy circular motion while moving a hand to the entrance of her core. One finger slid partway inside easily. She squirmed around him, her muscles clenching tightly. He added a second finger. It was a snug fit, and he upped the attention to her clit. Her body thrashed beneath him, and she wrapped her legs around the sides of his head. He pushed and felt her barrier break. His fingers sank deep into her. Vibrating tension in the clit in his mouth and the muscles surrounding his fingers told him it was time to cede his position.

"*Now, brother.*" Les withdrew and ducked from beneath her legs.

"Don't stop, damn it," she moaned, her hips bucking. "I'm almost there." In the candlelight, her eyes were glazed with lust.

"We know." Karl's voice was rough with desire. "We're not stopping, just trading places." He knelt between her legs and positioned his swollen cockhead at her entrance. "I'll take this slow, *liebchen.*"

"I don't want slow." She made a grab for his hips and pulled hard.

Les grinned. His groin ached and his cock felt like it was about to explode, but joy filled him as Karl sank his penis partway into their mate. He felt the other man's excitement, and it fed his own. The sound of their breathing quickened, loud in the candlelit room.

Megan threaded her legs around Karl's slender hips. He drew almost all the way out. Les saw her fluids gleaming on his shaft before Karl sank inside her body again, farther this time. Megan squirmed and cried out. Les felt her surprise at how big Karl's cock was, and then a flash of fear she wouldn't be able to contain him.

He moved close and fingered her clit. Karl understood and moved faster, driving himself home again and again. Her nubbin quivered beneath Les' fingers. He urged her with fingers and his mouth on hers to come. Once she did, the cock inside her would feel heavenly. Megan opened her mouth beneath his. Her clit grew even harder as he rubbed it, and then she dragged her mouth from his and shrieked as she orgasmed. Karl's cry thundered atop hers as he spasmed into her, juddering hard. Les' balls snugged against his body. His cock, sandwiched against Megan's hip, was so close to release he could've thought himself to a climax, but he held back.

Megan panted and moaned. Les gathered her close, noticing her legs were still wrapped firmly around Karl and she hadn't let go of his hips. "You were wonderful."

"Awesome, stupendous," Karl gasped.

"I-I almost panicked there for a minute," Megan's voice was muffled against his shoulder. "Karl's penis is so big. I had no idea I could stretch so far." She wrapped her arms around Les. "You haven't had a turn yet. Your cock feels like an iron bar pressed against me."

Karl pulled away from her body and lay on Megan's other side. He strung kisses down her hair and her forehead and cheek. "Thank you," he murmured. "That was the most wonderful, the most incredible…"

"Stop! This will go to my head." She laughed and wriggled between them. Her joy was contagious, but her movements reminded Les of the fire in his groin.

"If you're sore," he murmured, "I can take care of myself right now, and we can wait until you've rested a little before we complete the mate bond." Les bit his lip. Making that offer was hard, but he loved Megan and taking care of their new mate was more important than his pleasure.

Megan moved so she could meet his gaze. Her face was splotchy with sated passion. Long, blonde hair eddied around her. He'd never seen a woman look more beautiful and opened his mouth to tell her so, when she said, "I don't think I'll be any sorer. Besides, it wouldn't feel fair even if I brought you to a climax with my hand or mouth." She pushed herself up on her elbows. "I thought about this earlier, but then I guess I got swept away. We should've used a condom." Megan grinned sheepishly. "I figure it's unlikely, but are there any here?"

"Not needed," Karl said. "We control when we impregnate, and we're immune to human diseases. You will be too, for the most part, once the shifter magic takes hold."

"Oh, but that's wonderful." She rolled toward Les and wrapped her arms around him. "What are we waiting for? I actually think I can come again."

"Go for it," Karl urged. "She's incredible. Hot and tight. I came harder than I ever have before."

Les stopped thinking. He felt Megan's arousal in her open-mouthed kiss. Her breasts pressed against his chest, the nipples like stones. He held her close and put all his love and longing into their kiss. He felt Karl in his mind and welcomed him. Sharing this way made the sex even better. Megan moaned softly into his mouth. Her hips writhed against his erection, driving him mad.

Reluctantly, he broke their kiss. "Let's try it this way," he said. "I'm going to sit with my back against the wall. I want you to straddle me. Karl will be behind you. He's going to tickle your back door with his fingers. If you like the sensation, we can do more of it." Les settled his back against a pillow and opened his arms for her.

Megan's arousal filled the air with a musky perfume reminiscent of heather and spring wildflowers. She came to him and spread her legs, kneeling over him. He placed his hands on her hips and helped lower her onto his shaft. The feeling of her slick heat around him was almost unbearable. Les knew he wouldn't last long. She angled her head and licked one of his nipples. Liquid fire tracked right to his core and nearly blew the top of his head off.

"Ooh." She wriggled, her muscles caressing his shaft. "I like what Karl's doing. It's… interesting."

"Perfect," Karl sent. *"I'll just diddle her entrance where all the nerves are. Jesus! You're so hot, I don't understand why you haven't come."*

Les didn't understand it, either. His balls ached with denial. He moved Megan's hips and set a rhythm. She slid up and down his shaft, making little mewling noises. His breath came so fast, Les thought he might pass out, but he was damned if he wouldn't make her come before he did. He slid a hand between them and rubbed her clit. The combined stimulation of clit, ass, and pussy did it. Megan's muscles clenched hard, and she closed her teeth over his shoulder before she raised her head and shrieked her delight.

Les let himself go. He pumped into her once, twice, and then semen juddered out of him, hot and burning. He just kept coming, so shattered by the spasms his vision blurred.

Megan collapsed against him. Karl put his arms around them both. The deed was done. They were mated. Les wanted to jump up, shout his joy to the heavens, and dance around the room. The impossible had finally happened. He and Karl had a mate again. And what a mate she was. Gorgeous, strong-minded, a perfect complement to their family. In his deepest places, he vowed to make up for the family she'd been cheated out of as a youngster.

Les drew back and gazed tenderly at her. "I love you."

"As do I," Karl murmured. *"Ich liebe dich."*

"Ja, we will love and protect you forever," Les whispered.

"I love both of you too." She hesitated. "I'm surprised to hear myself say that. We barely know one another, but the words feel right on my tongue."

"They would. It's the magic of the mate bond," Les explained. "It speeds things up, makes it seem as if we've been together since the dawn of time."

Karl got to his feet and padded toward the door. "Where are you going?" Les asked.

"To wash my hands and get another bottle of wine. I'd say this calls for a round or two of toasts!"

∼

MEGAN WOKE to sunlight streaming through the uncurtained bedroom window. Les had an arm curved protectively over her, and Karl snugged up against her other side. She grinned and swallowed spontaneous laughter. The men were still asleep, and she didn't want to wake them. She thought she should pinch herself to make certain she hadn't dreamed everything that had happened since Alice, Jed, and the boys' car rolled to a stop in front of her the previous afternoon.

Oh my God. Alice and Jed.

Megan stared at the window and tried to figure out what time it was. Certainly past mid-morning by the angle of the light. Alice's words came back to her. *Sweetie, I'm betting you'll be sorry when you hear us pull into the driveway tomorrow because it'll mean you have to get out of bed.*

She wriggled out from between the men, driven by a full bladder and the need to know what time it was.

Les made a grab for her. "Up already?" He opened one sleepy eye and winked lasciviously.

"Not only up but leaving? You can't leave yet, sweetheart," Karl said.

"No," Les agreed. "We're nowhere near done with one another."

Megan rolled her eyes. "From the looks of things, we won't be done with one another for about fifty years. I've got to pee. Do either of you know the time? Jed and Alice and the guys will be back here fairly soon."

"Come to think of it—" Les rolled to his feet "—pissing's a great idea."

Megan just stared at him. She hadn't truly gotten a good look at his body the previous night in the lantern and candlelit cabin. "My God, you're incredible." She gazed at the graceful muscles lining arms and chest, his flat stomach, and the jut of hip bones. His cock was hard, and her gaze lingered there. She couldn't help it.

"Guess it's time for me to stand too." Karl moved off the bed and sashayed to Les' side. He raised his hands above his head and turned in a parody of a stripper. "What about me, love? Aren't I incredible too?"

Her throat grew dry. It didn't seem possible, but his body was even more perfect than Les'. His skin was a dusky bronze, where Les' was more golden, and his form leaner. "You're both pretty unbelievable." She shifted from foot to foot. "I still have to pee."

"Privy's out back," Les said. "You probably saw it yesterday, but you can't go out there barefoot."

Karl scooped a pair of knitted sock slippers with worn leather soles out of a corner and brushed the dust bunnies off them. He handed them to her. "Lean on me to put them on."

She slid her feet into the slippers. They were a little large, but they'd stay put. Megan blew kisses at the men and hurried outside, realizing instantly it was far too cold to be out of doors naked. She ducked into the privy, did what she needed to, and hustled back inside the cabin, but not before taking a moment to gawk at a day that looked more beautiful to her than any ever had before.

Guess it's because I'm really and truly in love for the very first time...

Karl had stirred the ashes of last night's fire and gotten a blaze going in the woodstove that also served as their only heat source. Les was busy at the sink with last night's dishes.

"Did either of you figure out what time it is?" she asked.

"Around ten-thirty." Les glanced over a shoulder and smiled.

"Jed and them won't show up much before noon." Karl secured the firebox door and straightened.

Les turned away from the dishes. Both men gazed expectantly at her.

Megan was acutely aware she wasn't wearing a thing except slippers. Worse, despite all her orgasms from yesterday, a familiar heat warmed her loins. "Is it always going to be like this?" She looked from one man to the other. "Where all we want to do is fuck?"

"Hot damn!" Les clapped his hands together. "I love it when she talks dirty."

"Yes." She flicked a hand toward his cock, jutting in front of him. "I can see that."

"We both love it, *liebchen*."

Karl pointed at his erection just to make certain she hadn't missed it. As if she could have. It was aimed right at her, just like one of Cupid's arrows.

Megan blew out a breath. "Okay, but only one round this time. I want to get the cabin looking better before Jed and Alice and the guys show up. Gosh, they'll think all we did was romp around in bed."

Les brayed laughter. Karl joined in. When they could talk again, Les said, "No matter what you do, sweetheart, they'll know we spent hours in bed because that's what newly mated shifters do."

"Plus, they'll smell it," Karl said. "No matter if you sluiced the cabin down with bleach or lime, they'd still smell all the pheromones from our mating heat."

Despite their abandon from the previous night, she felt suddenly shy as she sidled past the men and through the bedroom door. She'd loved the multiple points of stimulation where Les had been inside her with Karl tickling her anus. Maybe, if they only did one thing, they could repeat that… But both men needed release. An idea blossomed. Megan opened her mouth but couldn't get the words out. Talking about sex and asking for an act she'd always been taught was forbidden felt impossible.

The men's heat closed behind her. They folded her between them, kissing and fondling. Her nether regions ached, but it was a sweet ache, and she couldn't wait to feel a cock filling her again. Megan lost track of who was kissing and touching her. Kisses and caresses rained from all sides. She held a cock in both hands, sometimes unsure which belonged to whom.

Somehow they found themselves back on the bed. Les took up his seated position from the previous night, leaning against the wall. She knew what to do this time and straddled him, feeling her tissues stretch as she sank onto his cock. Karl's fingers teased her bud of an anus. The same sharp sensations shot through her. It was almost as if the men had read her mind. With a sudden shock, she remembered Alice. If a shifter mate could mind read, surely shifters could as well.

"Yes, sweetling." Les stopped kissing her long enough to talk. "We'll always know what you want."

"Sometimes before you do." Karl inserted a second finger into her ass. She wriggled against it, knowing she wanted more. The thought of having both cocks inside her was heady.

"Bear with us a minute." Les was panting. She sensed the men's arousal. All of them were on the verge of coming. He lifted her off his cock and back a little. Karl's cock sank deep into her vault. He thrust a few times and withdrew. Les settled her back onto his penis and reached for her clit.

This time it wasn't Karl's fingers, but the rounded head of his cock that pressed against her anal passage. His member was slick with her vaginal fluids. He slid in an inch or two and stopped. She flexed around him. It was a different sensation than the cock in her pussy, more intense in some ways. She arched her back and pushed against him. He understood and sank farther inside.

Les moved his cock in her pussy. Karl plumbed her from behind. Megan screamed. She hadn't believed pleasure this sharp and hot existed in the universe. When Les rubbed her clit, she shot over the edge so far she wondered if she'd ever stop coming. In the midst of her spasms, she felt the men release, first Karl and then Les. The men's passion was so palpable it rocked her to her core. To be able to give them pleasure as intense as what they gave her moved her to tears.

The men held her between them and murmured endearments in German. Megan could've stayed that way all day, held between the men who loved her, but she finally suggested that, maybe, they should get dressed.

"*Ja,* and I must wash." Karl's cock slipped from her anus. He got to his feet and headed for the kitchen.

Megan raised herself off Les' still-hard cock. "Doesn't it ever go down?"

"Apparently not when you're around. Aw, dammit!"

"What?" And then she heard it too. The sound of a car that had to mean Jed and Alice would be knocking at the door in moments. Or maybe they wouldn't bother to knock. The thought galvanized Megan into a leap from the bed. Semen ran down her legs. She wiped herself clean with a towel she found draped over a chair and loped to the front room to hunt for her discarded clothing.

CHAPTER 7

She barely had time to slither into her skirt and sweater when footsteps sounded on the porch steps. Someone knocked. Still naked, Karl dried his newly washed cock. Clutching the dishtowel, he strode toward the door.

"Your clothes," Megan squeaked.

"I'll put them on in a minute. Jed's our clan leader. It would be worse to keep him waiting than to answer the door this way. Besides—" Karl shot a grin her way "—we're all naked when we're wolves. Not much difference, really."

The front door popped open before Karl got to it. Jed strode in, a broad smile on his face. Alice, Bron, and Terin crowded after him. He sniffed audibly. "Smells like sex in here. Mate bond sex. What have you been up to?"

Megan felt herself turn bright red. Heat rolled off her in waves, and she spun to face the back of the cabin, uncomfortable with such a blatant discussion.

Alice closed her arms around Megan from behind. "Aw, honey. It's okay." Lips brushed her cheek. "Welcome to the pack, sister. I'm so glad things worked out."

Les strode in from the bedroom. From beneath her lowered

lids, Alice saw he'd at least put trousers on. "Thanks." She patted Alice's hands and tried to get her emotions under some sort of control. The other woman let go, and Megan half-turned back toward where the men were.

It wasn't that she was ashamed of what she and her new mates had done. No, it was more she wasn't used to public discussions about what happened between consenting adults. Cult members had plenty of sex, but they never talked about any of it.

There are new rules here. I'm going to have to figure out what they are and get used to them.

Jed covered the distance to Karl. He beckoned to Les and then to her. Confused, Megan didn't move. Alice gave her a little push.

"Jed just wants to bless your mating. Go on. I know he can be a little overbearing, but he doesn't mean a thing by it."

Jed snorted. "Gee, thanks, mated one. You're supposed to be on my side."

Alice glared at him, but Megan sensed she wasn't really angry. "You barreled in here like a damn locomotive and made our very newest pack mate uncomfortable."

Jed's blue gaze settled on her. "Did I?"

Megan squirmed under his stare. "Kind of. Um, it's really okay. All this will just take some getting used to."

"See," Alice pressed. "She's trying to cover up, but humans aren't used to open conversations about sex. It took me a while to get my head around everything after Bron and Terin showed up. When I knew they planned to fuck me too, I was shocked."

Jed chuckled. "I remember. You damn near got the both of us killed."

Alice strode to her mate's side and brushed her lips over his. "All's well that ends well. Come on over here, Megan. He doesn't bite, I promise."

She moved between Karl and Les, taking comfort from their solid energy flanking her. Alice retreated to where Bron and Terin stood near the door.

"Blessings on your mate bond." Jed laid a hand on each of their heads in turn. "May your union be fruitful." He bent forward and kissed Megan's forehead. "Thanks to you, Megan Galen, for being willing to join your life to ours. You've made Les and Karl very happy. I see it in their faces, and I read it in their minds."

"Blessings on your mating as well," Les said.

"Indeed," Karl concurred. "It's a pleasure to meet Alice."

Bron, Terin, and Alice closed on them, adding their good wishes and accepting their own congratulations on their newly formed mate bond.

"Any possibility of breakfast?" Jed asked at length. "We have things to discuss."

"Not the least of which is a fire that's growing closer," Bron cut in, his dark brows drawn into a worried line. "Maybe after we eat and talk, it would be a good idea to move the party into town."

Les turned to face him. "I smell smoke too. It's been there for days, but I agree it's getting nearer. We may evacuate at some point, but not until the threat's a lot more immediate than it is this minute."

"I'm going to find some clothes," Karl announced. "It's not all that warm in here."

"Megan and I can scare up some food," Alice said. "How about if you boys take your discussion outside?" She winked at Megan. "Shifter business. They usually don't let me listen—not to everything. I think they don't want to worry the little woman." Alice laughed, deep and throaty.

Megan joined her. The idea of either herself or Alice being described as *little women* was hilarious. Not at their nearly six feet heights. "It's all right," she said when she could talk again. "I probably wouldn't understand anything they talked about anyway. And I'm a pretty good cook."

"Great." Alice beamed at her. "Because I could burn water if someone didn't keep an eye on me."

"It's settled then." Jed stopped by Alice long enough to lay his cheek against hers and kiss her. Bron and Terin were already outside.

Les rose from the chair where he'd been putting on shoes and socks and trotted to Megan. He hugged her tight and whispered, "I love you."

Karl emerged from the bedroom with fresh clothes. He gave her a hug and a kiss before following Les out the door.

Megan's gaze swept the disorderly room. She picked up discarded clothing and dropped it onto a chair so she could fold it and put it away. "Wonder what they do for laundry out here?"

Alice rolled her eyes. "If it were my guess, I'd say they use a rock, sand, and a nearby creek." She moved in on Megan's project. "How about if I neaten up and you can get something to eat going. I'm hungry. Jed was in a big rush to get back out here, so he vetoed going out for breakfast."

"Why do you suppose—?" Megan quirked an inquisitive brow.

"I have no idea, but Jed's worried about something. Worried enough he's keeping his mouth shut so as not to alarm me."

Megan opened the few cupboards and quickly discovered she'd have to wash dishes to have something to serve breakfast on. She chucked more wood in the stove and ferried hot water to the kitchen sink in a pitcher. A quick search produced powdered detergent.

"Do you suppose the Hunters have something in mind?" Megan asked as she washed and rinsed dishes and silverware, pots and pans.

Alice glanced up from her clothes-folding project. "Probably." Her voice was bitter. "They always do. I don't understand why they can't just leave us alone." She shook her head. Dark hair spilled around her shoulders. "Want me to cut up some of that fruit we brought?"

"Sure." Megan bit her lower lip. She'd just found Les and Karl. If something happened to either one of them, it would tear her heart out.

~

Les stood in a semi-circle with Jed, Karl, Bron, and Terin off to one side of the yard and far enough away the women couldn't eavesdrop. "So it's really that bad?" he asked softly.

Jed nodded. "I tell you, they're adding to their ranks. This last attack in northern California could've been a disaster if we hadn't gotten wind of it."

"Are you considering an all-out war?" Karl asked.

"Not if we can avoid it," Jed replied. A muscle twitched in his jaw, and his hands were balled into fists. "I hate those bastards. If we could wipe every single one of them off the face of the earth, I'd do it in a heartbeat."

"Then why don't we just attack?" Terin broke in. "At the last shifter gathering, you four clan leaders decided we could kill Hunters instead of running from them."

Jed shook his head. "That decision wasn't unanimous. You'll recall we voted. The other three clan leaders thought killing was a grand idea. I cast the dissenting vote, yet we're bound by majority rule as we've always been."

"What are you afraid will happen?" Karl asked.

"Simple." Jed unfisted his hands and spread them before him. "There are more of them than there are of us. Plus, they can recruit volunteers. We're stuck with the numbers we have since the only way to make new shifters is by birthing them. In an out-and-out war, we'd lose."

Les clenched his teeth together. Jed's words were like a gut shot, but he recognized truth in them. "What do you propose?"

"For once, I don't know. That's the God's truth. My primary strategy, which was to just lay low, isn't working. Hunters are flushing us out of hiding. Pretty soon, absent places like this—" Jed waved an arm expansively "—there'll be nowhere for us to go."

"Is it this bad in Europe?" Karl asked.

"Worse," Bron muttered. "It was the damned war. Lots of us

retreated to our animal forms when the going got tough. It reminded people in the Old Country that we still existed."

"This is terrible." A sense of foreboding ripped through Les. "We have to keep the women safe. They depend on us."

Jed nodded. "That they do. Alice is one liberated gal, but even she got suckered by a Hunter before she met us."

"What happened to him?" Karl asked.

Bron shrugged. "Let's just say he met with an…unfortunate accident and lost his mind. He'll be in a mental ward for years."

Jed eyed his lieutenant askance. "You never actually told me what you did."

"And I'm not going to now," Bron retorted. "It's not important."

Les agreed. One less Hunter made for a better world, no matter how you cut it—or how it came to be. "So what do we do next?" he asked Jed.

"You and Karl need to find a more permanent place for yourselves now that you have Megan to consider."

"But we've lived here for years," Les protested. "What's wrong with it?"

"I've been considering the same issue," Karl said quietly. "It's one thing for us to rinse our clothes in the creek and turn into wolves when we don't feel like bathing. Or take cold showers when we're human. But we can hardly expect Megan to take to such a primitive existence."

"Pioneer women had it worse," Les mumbled.

"Yes." Karl eyed his pack mate. "Many died in childbirth, living in crude conditions not unlike what we left in Europe."

Les shut his eyes. Pain sluiced through him. He couldn't stand to lose another mate to anything. Not Hunters. Not childbirth. Not accidents. "Point taken. I love this place, but I want our mate close to modern medicine when our children are born."

"Why not move near enough to town you could at least get electricity?" Jed suggested smoothly. "Surely you could find something that has this remote feel but a few more modern conveniences as well."

Les cocked his head to one side. "We could've gotten electricity here, but it's about as unreliable as the phone service. Never felt worth it. And moving closer to civilization isn't going to solve the Hunter problem. We'll be more visible, so by my way of thinking, that part of things will only get worse."

"You're right." Jed nodded curtly. "I'm deluding myself by pretending this problem is controllable. Every time I try to talk my way around the Hunter incursion, I end up tearing my hair out. We need to kill them, every last fucking one. But we've got to find some subtle way, so their deaths won't be pinned on us."

"Like the ones we took care of a few days back." Karl spoke low.

"Exactly," Jed concurred. "Except most of us don't have a handy multi-level cave system nearby to stash and burn bodies."

"It was convenient—once we located it," Les agreed.

Jed flashed a meaningful look Karl's way. "Les told me about the cave, but you've got to shield your thoughts better, brother. I see the cave in them clear as if I was there. If I can read your mind, so can some of the telepathic Hunters."

"Damn!" Karl reddened. "Sorry. That's always been one of my weak areas."

"Awareness is the first step to change." Jed reached across the circle and patted Karl's arm. He blew out a tense breath. "At this point, we need to call another meeting of the clans."

"But we just had one a few months ago," Bron protested.

"True enough," Jed agreed. "It would be most unusual to meet again this soon, but we need a strategy we can all integrate into local action plans. If the bear clan is slaughtering Hunters outright and we're killing them surreptitiously, no one benefits. We all need to agree to do the same thing. And—" Jed let his gaze linger on each man for a long moment "—we have to be stealthy. If we're not, I fear we're doomed."

"What do we tell the women?" Terin asked.

"Nothing." Les bit off the word and then looked apologetically at Jed. "Sorry, boss. That's your call, not mine."

"In this case, I agree with you," Jed said. "No point in alarming them over something they have no control over. Either myself or Terin or Bron will get in touch with you when there's a meeting date and time set. It needs to be soon, and unlike most of our gatherings, everyone needs to come. We've always operated on democratic principles. One shifter, one vote."

"You can let our kinfolk up here know when they show up day after tomorrow," Les said.

Bron and Terin exchanged glances. "That's our job," Terin said. "Jed's going to take Alice back to California soon. She has to get back to work, and it's safer for her there."

Bron smiled crookedly. "The best place to hide is usually in plain view."

Les turned the words over in his mind. They made a great deal of sense. Alice wasn't running from something like Megan. His upper lip drew back in a snarl.

"What?" Jed glanced at him.

"Nothing. I was just thinking about Megan. She's on the run from a cult in Calgary because they discovered blood sacrifices are a huge thrill. But we can keep her safe from them."

"Of course we can," Karl cut in.

"Just because you're capable of protecting your mate from humans, who no doubt want her back," Jed said slowly, "the last thing you need is a confrontation where what you are becomes visible."

"We understand that—" Les began.

"No." Jed raised his voice. "You don't. You're newly mated and not thinking clearly. What you need to do is take your mate and move far away from Calgary and that bunch of cult-weirdoes who might do something stupid to make sure she doesn't spill the beans about their activities."

"Maybe he's right," Karl said, looking thoughtful.

Maybe he is, Les thought, *but I don't want to think about it.*

The notion of leaving a homestead he'd carved out of the forest devastated him. He loved these woods as both man and wolf, and he'd started over so many times, he didn't want to again. But he didn't want to put their mate at risk, either.

Silence fell over the small group. When Les glanced up, everyone was looking at him. "I'll consider your advice," he told Jed.

"Yes," Karl said meaningfully. "We'll talk about it, and we'll find out where Megan would like to settle before we make a final decision."

Guilt smote Les. Naturally, they'd have to talk with their mate. He shook himself from head to toe, much as he did when he was a wolf, and met Karl's even, dark gaze. "Of course we will," he said. "Thanks for keeping our family on track."

"You're welcome."

"I smell food," Terin said hopefully.

"So do I." Bron nodded and clasped his hands together in anticipation. "Jed hustled us out of Rocky Mountain House before we could get breakfast."

"Wouldn't have been so bad," Terin grumbled, "except we sort of missed dinner too."

"For the love of Pete, would you two stand down? When we're wolves, sometimes we go days without eating." Jed tossed his hands dismissively into the air. "We're a pretty grim-looking lot. Let's put on better faces before we go inside to face our mates."

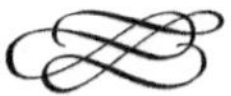

CHAPTER 8

"What a wonderful meal. It was just perfect!" Jed laid his fork down and beamed at Alice and Megan.

"Smile at her." Alice hooked a thumb toward Megan. "She did all the cooking. I just followed her instructions."

"You have other...attributes, sweetheart." Jed winked. "So I'll just keep on smiling at you both."

"Thanks." Megan took a sip of tea she'd made from dried herbs the men had in canisters. "I did the best I could, but I swear if it hadn't been for all the food you brought with you yesterday, we'd have been in sad shape." She eyed Les and Karl. "What were the two of you eating? All I found was a couple cans of pork and beans and another of tomatoes."

Les looked uncomfortable. Karl was suddenly very busy bending to scratch one of his legs.

"The lady asked you a question," Terin said, his amber eyes glittering mischievously. "If you aren't going to answer her, I will."

Truth dawned. Megan bit back a laugh. "Don't tell me that every time you get hungry, you just turn into wolves and hunt something down."

"That's exactly what they do," Jed said. "Game's probably plentiful around here, so that strategy makes excellent sense. But that was before you came into their lives." He skewered Les and Karl with his sharp, blue gaze. "One more reason to move nearer a supply point. Even if you drop fresh game on the porch for Megan to dress and cook, you can't expect her to live on meat."

"I could try." Megan felt defensive of her mates. "It's too late in the year now, but next spring we could plant a vegetable garden, and I could do some canning." Les gazed at her with such a look of gratitude, it warmed her to her toes. Karl reached across the table and squeezed her hand.

"Okay," Jed said implacably, "you can spend the cold months nearer town and return here in the spring if that's what the bunch of you decide."

Apparently he'd made up his mind that Les and Karl's home site was too primitive for her. Megan girded herself to argue.

"They could winter with us," Alice suggested brightly. "That would kill a whole bunch of birds with one stone. Megan could figure out her shifter magic, and you'd all be close for whatever sort of Armageddon I sense coming." She smiled disingenuously. "You know, the one you're not telling me about."

"You can be a real pill when you don't agree with what's going on." Bron ruffled her dark hair.

"Like you can't?" Alice retorted and smoothed her hair back behind her shoulders.

"That might not be a bad idea," Karl said thoughtfully.

"What?" The conversation had gone so many directions, Megan felt confused.

"Spending the winter in California." Karl's mouth twitched into half a smile.

"You've got to be kidding." Les' eyes widened, and he looked nonplussed.

"No. I'm not. There are lots of good reasons," Karl persisted.

Les opened his mouth to argue.

"How about if you hash this out as a family unit, and we'll check in with you later?" Terin suggested.

Jed nodded. "Good idea. We'll head back to Red Deer. We're going to buy another car and a few supplies for my boys, and then we'll stop back by here tomorrow morning. After the clan gathering in the evening day after tomorrow, Alice and I are returning to California. Bron and Terin will stay with the troops here and make sure the clan's all flying the same direction. If they have time before the next gathering, they'll move west and do the same thing through British Columbia and then swing down the west coast, alerting everyone before they come home."

"Who made that plan?" Alice's jaw clenched. Sparks flew from her green eyes.

"I know it's hard to be apart." Bron leaned toward her and draped an arm around her shoulders. She shook him off.

"Seriously, how could the three of you have decided something so momentous without even consulting me?"

"We didn't want to alarm you, sweetheart." Jed reached for her too. Alice pushed back from the table and scrambled to her feet. Her chair wobbled precariously, but she caught it before it fell over.

With her nascent shifter magic, Megan felt an energy field flow from Jed's raised hands. Alice tossed her head.

"Stop that. Save your compulsion spells for someone else."

Suddenly, Les was on one side of Megan and Karl the other. They guided her upright and out the cabin door. "We need to leave them alone to work this out," Les murmured low into her ear.

Megan nodded. "Maybe it will give us a few minutes alone to talk too," she whispered back and followed the men to a rickety bench leaning against a storage shed about thirty feet from the cabin. A weak autumn sun warmed her as she snuggled between her mates. Breakfast had been good. She'd made a large fruit salad with eggs and toasted cheese sandwiches. Her belly was full, and

Megan decided it was impossible to be annoyed with anyone on such a beautiful day. The first full day of her new life as a shifter mate.

Les turned her face so she met his gaze. "What do you want to do about a place to live?"

Megan considered it. "Right now, I'm so head-over-heels ga-ga over both of you, I'd probably agree to anything, but living on pork and beans or fresh game would get old really fast. Standup baths in the kitchen would too. And I imagine it gets hella cold here during the winter. The cabin's not all that weatherproof..." Her voice trailed off.

Karl wove an arm around her before he spoke. "We're coming to those same conclusions. You're as much of a surprise to us as we are to you, and it takes time to think these things through. Following Jed to California could work. It would get you away from the Garden of Edeners long enough for them to forget about you. It would also get us out from under one more winter here. And away from the fire threat if it continues to spread. Come spring after the snow melts, we'll come back here and figure out if we could make this cabin work as our home or if we need to move closer to Red Deer. There's not much at Rocky Mountain House."

"If we drove to California—" Les blew out a breath and sucked in another "—we'd need to buy a better car. And we'd have to batten this place down for winter, so it would still be standing when we came back."

"Uh, I hate to be any trouble, and I do have a bit of my own money, but I need almost everything," Megan cut in. "Clothes, toiletries, underwear, shoes. About all I tucked in my bag were my hair and tooth brushes."

"That's easy enough. There are haberdasheries in Red Deer where you can buy whatever you're missing," Karl said.

Les shot him a pointed look. "We'll buy her whatever she needs."

"I couldn't let you—"

"You can and you will." Les laid a finger over her mouth. "We're your mates. That means we'll take care of you."

"He's right," Karl said. "Save your money for something frivolous." He grinned. "I'm sure we'll find lots of indulgences in California."

"Won't I need a passport?" she asked.

Les clapped a hand to his forehead. "We'll all need them. Ours expired a while back."

"That's an understatement. When did we get them? 1929?" Karl repositioned himself so she got full benefit of the sun's warmth.

"Somewhere around then," Les said, "and they're only good for five years."

"Does it take very long?" Megan asked.

"I don't think so," Karl replied. "Last time, we just dropped by the courthouse."

Les knitted his brows together. "Did you bring any identification?"

Megan nodded. "I had the presence of mind to do that, so I have my birth certificate and high school graduation diploma. And the papers from the orphanage."

Something passed between Les and Karl just at the edges of her consciousness. "Are you two talking to each other somehow?"

Les nodded. "Your magic is taking root. Soon we'll all be able to communicate telepathically."

She straightened between the men and looked from one to the other. "Well, since I can't interpret your mental speech quite yet, what were you saying?"

Karl snorted. "You'll be hell on wheels once you can listen in. We realized we were talking about going to California as if it were a done deal. But we hadn't actually asked you if it was what you wanted."

A warm glow began in her belly. It felt good to be cared about. She could get used to it. "I think it would be a grand adventure. I've never been outside Alberta, and I've always wanted to travel."

Les brushed his thumb across her lips. "Guess that settles it. We'll be vagabonds for a while."

Megan's brow furrowed. "I know you love it here, Les. Are you all right with us leaving?"

He nodded thoughtfully. "Yes, I believe I am. My wolf loves it here because it's easy for him to romp and be wild and free. There wasn't any reason to corral my animal nature, so I've indulged myself for a long time."

"Me too," Karl said. "But I'm ready to be human more of the time."

"Then it looks as if we have a plan, at least for the next few months." Excitement burned through her. Not only did she have two men wanting to attend to her every need, she'd get to see a bit of the world as well.

"Yes, we all agree," Les murmured. "That's important. We're a partnership. It will grow with time as we nurture the love and trust."

Megan looked away. She wanted to ask if they'd shift for her but felt unaccountably shy.

Karl got to his feet and unbuttoned his shirt. Les followed suit and pulled a threadbare sweater he'd put on before breakfast over his head.

"What are you doing?" Megan glanced about. Surely they weren't planning to make love out in the open like this when Jed and the others could come trooping through the cabin door at any moment.

"You'll see." Les' green eyes sparkled.

In moments, he and Karl were naked. The air shimmered around them, taking on a glittery multi-toned hue. When it cleared, two strongly built timber wolves stood before her. Their eyes were the same: Karl's so dark it was hard to make out the pupils and Les' green as fine emeralds. Karl's pelt was nearly black while Les looked more like timber wolves she'd seen in pictures. His fur shaded from black to gray to brown, with splotches of white on his chest.

"Ooooh." She sank to the ground between them and buried her hands in their coats. They rolled against her and licked any exposed skin they could find. "You're just beautiful," she murmured.

"Yes, we are, aren't we," sounded in her mind.

"Oh my God, I actually heard you," she squealed. "Which one of you said that?"

"Me." The black wolf nosed her with a cold, wet snout.

"Try sending your thoughts to us." Les' mind voice was deeper than Karl's.

"How do I do that?"

"Imagine you're talking, but keep the words inside your head. We should be able to hear you."

It took a few tries, but Megan found the frequency where they could hear her. The wolves gamboled about the clearing while she practiced talking to them, and she marveled at how striking they were. Muscles rolling beneath shiny fur, they were grace incarnate as they leapt and spun in the air.

The house door slammed open. Bron and Terin raced into the yard. "What a grand idea," Bron cried and stripped off his clothes.

"Bet I can beat you, brother," Terin shouted.

Megan just laughed, deep, heartfelt laughter from her belly as Terin and Bron turned into wolves. Bron was dark like Karl, where Terin had a reddish pelt to match his hair.

"Well," sounded from the porch. "I'll be damned if I'm the only shifter who's still human."

Jed must've dropped his clothes on the porch because a huge, grey and silver timber wolf arced through the air, landing on the others. A snarling, scrapping match ensued, but Megan could tell they were playing with each other.

Megan got to her feet and walked to where Alice had settled

on the porch steps. "They're amazing." She sat next to the other woman.

"They sure are," Alice concurred. "Sort of takes your breath away."

"Did you get everything worked out?"

Alice smiled softly. "Yeah. I can be a real bitch, but the guys tolerate me. They know how worried I am about them."

"We decided to accept your offer of joining you in California—if it's still okay, that is."

Alice clapped her hands together. "Splendid. I told Jed it would be the very best thing, but he was certain Les would never leave here. How'd you talk him into it?"

"I didn't. He and Karl started looking at all the ways they'd gotten used to living, especially through the winters, and decided I'd be miserable."

Alice slitted her eyes at Megan. "Would you have been?"

Megan grinned sheepishly. "Right about now, I'd have agreed to anything, but yeah, I'm sure always being cold—except when we were in bed—and not having a proper bathroom or access to a grocery store would've gotten old really, really fast. Remember a couple hours ago when we were cooking? We would've been out of luck for breakfast if it weren't for all your groceries."

"I'm absolutely delighted." Alice clapped her hands together. "When are you coming? We have a huge house. More than enough room for everyone. It will be grand to have another woman around. You know, I've never really had a girlfriend…" Alice's face reddened and her voice faltered. "Sorry, I'm getting ahead of myself here."

Megan turned and hugged Alice. "No you're not. I've never had many friends, either. And it's looking as if the ones from the cult I ran away from weren't really any kind of friends at all. More like acquaintances."

Alice bent close to Megan's ear. "I haven't said anything because I didn't want to hurt the guys' feelings, but I believe one of the reasons it's been so hard for them to find mates is because being a shifter mate is pretty isolating. It's not like you can go out for lunch or coffee with your girlfriends and share much of anything about your life."

Megan thought about that; it made sense. For women like herself and Alice, who were independent and used to being alone, life as a shifter mate fit. But most women relied on a network of others for support. "Maybe we could start sort of like a group of us," Megan said tentatively. "There must be lots of shifter mates scattered about, and we could reach them telepathically if we were close enough."

"Depending on how strong their magic is, we could reach them over some pretty hefty distances," Alice concurred. "That's a really good idea. I tried to suggest something similar to Jed, but he didn't think it was important." Her mouth curved into a soft smile. "He believes he can fill all my needs."

Megan quirked a brow. "What an opening. I can't resist. Well, does he?"

Alice laughed. "Between the three of them, I've discovered needs I never knew I had before. But it's not the same as having girlfriends."

"Since neither of us has had much practice in that regard, maybe we could figure out the girl pal thing together. Once we have it down, we can broaden our circle."

"I'd like that." Alice's green eyes glowed. "Oh, look. The boys are done playing."

Megan gazed across the clearing. Five naked men emerged from a glowing mist and trotted to their respective piles of clothing. Jed chugged up the porch steps to find his. "About ready to go, sweetheart?" he asked as he pulled on underwear.

"Sure." Alice got to her feet and walked up the few steps to stand next to her mate. "I have wonderful news! They're joining us in California."

"Really? Hey, Megan, I'm impressed. How'd you talk Les into leaving?"

She rolled her eyes. "Alice asked me the same thing. I didn't talk him into anything. In fact, I don't think anyone could talk either Les or Karl into something they truly didn't want to do."

"Perspicacious of you, my dear." Jed strode down the steps with Alice on his arm. He patted Megan's shoulder as he passed her. "We'll be back tomorrow."

"Hey, boss." Les walked up to them. "Maybe we could caravan back to the States with you. I don't know how much of a hurry you're in, but all we need to do is spend a long day in Red Deer getting supplies and passports, and then we'd be ready to go."

"I think we could do that." Jed grinned. "It would be fun to have company."

"Great!" Karl joined the group and thumped Les' back. "It's settled then. We'll drive into Red Deer early tomorrow and meet back with everybody here at the cabin tomorrow night to prepare for the local clan gathering the next day. Once it's over, we can leave. All but Bron and Terin—" He stopped short, glancing at Alice and Jed. "Sorry, I have no idea how that ended up."

Alice rolled her eyes. "Even though I'll miss my mates, Jed's right to leave them here to make certain everyone shows up for the next multi-clan gathering."

"Thank you, sweetheart." Jed kissed Alice's cheek.

Megan wrapped her arms around herself to contain her anticipation. Two more days and she'd be on her way to California with her mates. She said a silent prayer of thanks that she'd taken a chance the day before and gotten into Alice and Jed's car. If she hadn't been so alone and so desperate, she probably would have turned them down.

Somebody's watching out for me. I need to follow my instincts more often.

CHAPTER 9

Megan stood between Les and Karl as they watched Jed's car pull slowly out of the rutted, dirt driveway. Once it was well on its way, Les turned to Karl. "You looked at the truck lately?"

"Nope. It's so long since we've driven it, the gas has probably separated into water and whatever else is in it."

"I don't know much about cars," Megan said. "Is that a bad thing?"

Karl nodded. "Yeah, we'll have to drain the tank, strain the gas, and pour it back in. Not that big a deal."

Les placed an arm around Megan's shoulders, drew her close, and kissed her forehead. "Will you be all right for a little while? We need to make sure the truck can get us all the way to Red Deer tomorrow."

"We've been planning to sell it for years," Karl chimed in, "but we so rarely go anywhere, it was hard to justify the expense for a newer vehicle." He closed on her other side and laid his cheek next to hers.

"Of course I'll be okay. It will give me a chance to clear up the mess from breakfast and get the dishes done and back in the cupboards. I assume we'll want to eat later, so we'll need them."

Les reached around her and elbowed Karl. "Next thing she'll be telling us we need more dishes."

Megan wriggled from under both men's arms and placed her hands on her hips. "You need some serving bowls and more silverware too. And an icebox, or maybe a springhouse or something to keep perishable food cold."

"Bro." Karl jabbed Les back. "Our carefree days of batching it are definitely over. No more, *hey, I'm hungry, let's go kill something.*"

"Ewww." Megan wrinkled her nose.

"If you were a wolf, you'd understand." Les laughed. "I love you, Megan. You're worth making sacrifices for."

She shook her head. "I'll be damned if eating inside on dishes is a sacrifice. Maybe Alice and I can socialize you two on the way to California."

"Looking forward to it, sweetheart." Karl blew her a kiss and hooked an arm through Les'. "Come on, let's get this show on the road. I don't like getting greasy any more than you do."

Megan trotted up the steps and into the house. She stood in the doorway and surveyed the small cabin. Absent electricity and a more reliable source of heat, it would be hard to make it livable year-round. And it would take a lot of work. Daylight shone through chinks between the logs in the cabin's walls. She started gathering dirty dishes and then realized she'd need hot water, so she stoked the fire that, mercifully, hadn't quite died yet.

As she worked, Megan found herself laughing, grinning like a besotted fool, and singing. Happiness, true happiness, was such a foreign emotion, she was nearly drunk on the sensation. She was just drying and stacking the last of the dishes when Les ducked inside. His hands were grease streaked. He reached for her dishtowel, but she snatched it away. "No way. Wash your hands with some of that Fels-Naptha over by the sink and hot water. It was caked pretty badly, but I chipped some off to use for the dishes."

Les just stared at her. And then he threw back his head and howled with laughter. "Christ! For a minute you sounded so much like my mother or my aunts, I thought I was back in Germany." He walked dutifully to the sink and scrubbed his arms to the elbows, rinsing them in her used dishwater. "Clean enough?" He held out his forearms. They dripped water on the floor, but he seemed oblivious to the mess he was making.

Megan made a sound between a grunt and a snort. It was so unladylike, it shocked her. "Use fresh cold water from the pump. I see soap scum. Then I'll dry your arms. How's the truck coming along?" She strode to his side and toweled his arms dry once he'd rinsed them again. The detergent had cut through all the grease, but his skin had reddened from the harsh chemicals.

"Not so good. Karl's a better mechanic than I am, and there's really only room for one of us in the shed with the truck, so I left him to it. We both decided you'd been by yourself long enough." He glanced around. "Cabin looks great. Thanks for clearing up from breakfast."

She cocked her head to one side. "What would you have done if I wasn't here?"

Les shrugged. "Oh, we'd have gotten around to washing dishes eventually."

"What? Days, weeks?"

He grinned, making him look like a mischievous urchin. "Somewhere between those two options."

"I suspected as much. You need me."

"No one's contesting that, darling." He closed his arms around her. His warmth and bulk felt solid and reassuring. Les tipped her chin up and settled his mouth over hers. Desire knifed through her. Megan's nipples pebbled into peaks. She wound her arms around him and opened her mouth to his kiss. In moments, they were panting and grinding their bodies together. The jut of his erection pressed into her belly.

She broke their kiss. "Don't we need to get Karl?"

"He's working on the car."

"Yes, I know that, but I don't want him to feel cheated."

Les smiled at her. "You are such a gem. He and I talked about this. He's sharing our lovemaking through the mental link we have. Later on, when he's either finished or it's too dark to work, you and he can have some one-on-one time."

"What happens if he can't fix the car?"

"I'll get hold of Jed and he'll have to give us a lift into Red Deer so we can buy another one." His green eyes darkened as he gazed at her. "Let's not talk about cars."

She ran her tongue over her upper lip and was rewarded when his cock jumped against her belly. "Let's not talk about anything." She turned her face up for another kiss. He didn't disappoint her. Les licked at the seam between her lips, and she opened her mouth to his questing tongue. Megan loved the way he tasted, sweet like well-aged port.

He ran his hands slowly down her back and cupped her buttocks, pulling her against his erection. Megan couldn't wait to feel him against her body skin-to-skin. She pushed his shirt up and out of the way and then her sweater, never breaking their kiss. His skin was silken against hers; he radiated heat and need. She moved a hand from his back, squeezed it between them, and tweaked his nipples. He growled low in the back of his throat. Encouraged, she moved her mouth lower, down his neck and chest until she could suckle him.

"Not fair," he panted. "I'm supposed to be doing that to you."

She gave his nipple one more lascivious lick and straightened. "These clothes have to go." With a yank, she pulled her sweater over her head and unfastened her skirt. There wasn't any underwear in the way today because she'd been in such a rush getting dressed.

Les took a step back, fingers working the buttons of his shirt. His gaze swept her from head to toe. "You're so lovely. I don't think I've ever seen such a fine pair of breasts. They're perfect, so full and lush. And those incredible long legs and your hips. Darling, you were made for childbearing. And for loving." His shirt fell onto the floor. He unzipped his pants and pushed them partway down his legs. His cock jutted from his body, heavy with a promise of delight.

Her pussy ached for him. "See you in bed." She winked and turned for the bedroom.

"Not so fast, sweetheart." Les toed out a chair, awkward because of the pants he hadn't fully removed, and sat. "Come sit on me, but face away. That way I can reach around your body and caress you while we make love." He pumped a hand slowly up his shaft. "Hurry. I can't wait to feel you around me."

Megan gazed at him. He was so beautiful with his tawny hair spilling around him and splotches of color from arousal on his face and chest. The muscles in his chest tensed as he worked his penis. Watching him touch himself thrilled her. She squared her shoulders and dipped a hand between her legs, never taking her gaze from him.

He groaned. "Yes, darling. Touch yourself, but don't come. Just let me watch you."

"Like I'm watching you?" Her breath came fast, throat so thick with desire it was hard to breathe. Her clit stiffened under her fingers; she was close.

"I don't need to read your mind to see how puckered your nipples are or the rosy color on your chest and face. I'm close too. Come straddle me."

She walked to him and turned around. He placed his hands on her hips and guided her onto his erection. Then he reached around and settled one hand on a nipple and the other between her legs. She reached for the table's edge to stabilize herself and rose slowly until just the tip of him tickled her opening. She tightened her muscles around his cockhead again and again until he gripped her hips and pulled her all the way down onto his shaft.

Megan wanted to come, needed to. She was so close. Her hips

moved of their own volition. Les rubbed her clit. The sensations began in her belly and spiraled outward as a long, lazy orgasm shook her to her core. Somewhere in the midst of her climax, she felt Les judder inside her.

Karl dove into her mind urging both of them on. *"My God, the two of you are so hot. I'm jacking myself. My cock is huge. Hot. Hard. Yessss... Almost there. Almost. Coming. Coming. Aieeeeeee."*

Karl's heat translated through their mind link. She dropped a hand to the one Les still had on her clit and urged him to rub her quick and hard. A second orgasm followed on the heels of her first. Her pussy clenched around the cock inside her, milking it, glorying in the amazing sensations shooting through her.

She sank back against Les, panting. "Wow! I didn't think I could get any higher, but hearing Karl really did it for me."

Les flexed his cock inside her. "Yeah, got me going again too, but I really need to get out there and try to help him. We'll lose the light in a few hours."

She lifted herself off him, turned, and bent so she could brush her lips over his. "That's fine. I'm going to heat more water, wash out some clothes, and do the best I can to bathe and wash my hair."

He got to his feet and started pulling on his discarded clothes. "There's always the shower out back. It's pretty comfortable out there today."

"But the water's cold."

He ruffled her hair. "Yup. I can warm pots and tubs of water, but I never figured out how to warm water that's flowing."

Fondness welled in her. "Never mind. I'll manage."

"Maybe when you're done," he sounded hopeful, "you might think about something for supper."

"Of course. Good thing we have something to eat it off of."

He rolled his eyes and chugged out the door. She thought about getting dressed but decided it made more sense to clean herself first. Once that was done, she could wrap herself in the robe she'd seen hanging on the back of the bedroom door and work on laundry.

~

LES STRODE INTO THE SHED. "How's it going?"

Karl winked. "Pretty hot, if you ask me. Now if you'd just taken her to bed, I might've been able to concentrate, but no, you had to encourage her to fondle herself and have her facing where I could see everything." He patted his crotch through the front of a pair of grease-stained coveralls he'd pulled over his clothes.

Les eyed his hands. "Did you get grease on your dick?"

Karl punched him in the arm. "Probably. It'll wash off."

"Seriously, how's the truck?"

"At least I figured out what's wrong. No spark. I'd just fixed that part when things inside the house got too intense to ignore."

"Do you want me to try to turn it over?"

"Yeah. Don't choke it. I've got enough gas in the carburetor to explode."

"Erk. That's comforting." Les clambered behind the wheel, made a few adjustments, and turned the key. The engine sputtered to life. "What now?" he called over the rumble of the engine.

"Back it outside and let it run for a while."

Les put it in gear and then remembered he hadn't looked behind the truck. "Anything behind me?"

"Let me look. Nope, all clear." Karl tugged the rickety shed doors open wider.

Les coaxed the 1925 International Harvester truck out into the sunshine and took a good look around its cab. He groaned. It was filthy. Something like a mouse nest filled the passenger foot well. Dust and cobwebs covered every surface. He set the brake and jumped down. "Good thing we have time."

"Hey, I'm just glad we got it going."

"Me, too, but that was only the first part. I'm going after a bucket and a few rags. We can't have Megan in here the way it is right now."

Karl stepped onto the running board and peered through a very dirty window. "Mmph. Guess you're right. I was going to wash the windows, but the rest of it needs some love too. What's our mate up to?"

"Bath and laundry."

Karl quirked a brow. "Do you suppose she'd mind washing out a few things for me? I don't have anything clean for this trip."

Les snorted. "I was planning to just buy new clothes, but you can ask her. I don't want her to feel like we're taking advantage of her good nature, though." He turned to Karl. "I still can't believe how lucky we were to find her."

"Know what you mean." A fierce look blazed in the depths of his dark eyes. "I want to gather her close and love her and protect her—forever."

"Yeah, part of me wishes we were still in the Old Country a few hundred years ago, and we could shower her with servants and everything she'd ever want."

Karl looked thoughtful. "There's plenty of money. We could move to a town somewhere and hire household help."

"You're not thinking. We're fugitives, remember? All we'd need would be a nosy housekeeper to turn us in to the Hunters."

"Yeah. I suppose you're right." Karl disappeared into the shed and returned with a rag. He wiped his hands but didn't make a dent in the greasy streaks peppering them. "It's not that I forgot, not exactly, but I've just been so ecstatic since we found Megan, it was easy to push reality aside."

"Hi, guys!" Megan strode toward them wearing Les' blue, terrycloth robe belted about her slender waist. "I've got soap in the wash kettle. Do either of you have clothes you'd like washed?"

"You don't have to." Les opened his arms, and she walked into them.

"I know I don't, but I want to."

Karl nodded and gave up trying to lever the grease off his hands. "If you're sure it's not an imposition, I have a few things." He reached for her.

Megan quirked a brow and shook her head. "I'd love to have you hold me—after your hands are clean. Truck sounds promising." She hooked her thumb at the idling vehicle. "How about if you come inside, do some work on those hands, and then you can sort what you want me to wash."

"Sure." Karl turned to Les. "Set the idle down and make sure you can start it again."

"Will do. I'll be inside presently to get what I need to clean this beast up at bit." Les smiled as he watched his pack brother and their mate walk into the cabin. He put the old truck through its paces, satisfied when he turned the engine off that it would get them to Red Deer. When he got out of the truck, he wrinkled his nose, sniffing. Smoke. He'd nearly forgotten about the forest fire, but it was definitely moving closer.

It doesn't matter. We'll be out of here soon.

The specter of their cabin burning to the ground didn't bother him as much as it had before Megan entered their lives. It was looking unlikely they'd be living here anyway, and they could always replace the few things in the cabin if a fire swept through and demolished it.

CHAPTER 10

Megan leaned into both her mates. After an early dinner, they'd settled on the bench near the barn to watch what turned out to be a spectacular sunset. Though the colors were gradually fading, the sky still held tinges of violet, teal, and a rare pink. She gestured skyward. "Sounds kind of hokey, but it's like nature is celebrating our mating."

Les nuzzled her neck. "You never know, darling, maybe it is."

She straightened and disentangled their arms from around her. "I have a question. It's a serious one."

Two sets of eyes focused intently on her. "Ask us anything." Karl made an encouraging hand gesture.

"Yes. Anything at all," Les seconded.

"Are either of you sad about leaving this cabin even for a little while? You've made a life for yourselves here. For that fact, how about not being able to romp as much as wolves? Will you miss that too?"

Karl nodded slowly. "I'll miss some of it, but it's a life we created for ourselves when we didn't have any other choices." He paused a beat. "Missing something and wishing things could stay the same are two different things. I wouldn't trade having found you for staying here for the next million years."

"Well, said, brother," Les murmured. "Part of it is we retreated here when things heated up with the Hunters. So far, it's provided sanctuary, and while I'm grateful for that, I can move on." He narrowed his green eyes. "You asked for a reason. What is it?"

She looked away, suddenly uncomfortable. "I guess I didn't want you to give up too much on account of me. I love both of you, and I want you to be happy too. I could figure out how to make things work here—if that was truly important to you."

Les tilted her chin up with a finger so she had to look at him and Karl. "Sweetheart. You're the most important thing in our world. We want you to be content and comfortable—"

"Yes," Karl cut in. "We've lived lots of places. So many, we know it's not the place but the people around us that make a difference."

"But what about shifting, being wolves?" she persisted.

"We'll still do that," Les said.

"Maybe not as much," Karl added. "But one of the most important reasons to remain in our animal forms was to keep the possibility of forming a mate bond alive. Now that we have a mate, it's not a critical as it once was."

Megan digested his words, considering them. "So you never gave up finding someone like me."

Emotion flashed over the men's faces. "Of course not," Karl said.

"How could we?" Les demanded. "Our lives weren't complete after we lost Breta." He closed his arms around her. "We love you, Megan."

"And we're amazed and grateful you've graced our lives," Karl murmured, closing on her for a hug.

Les covered her other side and held her against him. It felt awkward with the three of them lined up along the bench, so she stumbled to her feet with one man on each side. Warm kisses rained down her head and neck, and Karl snaked his tongue into her ear.

"Did we answer your questions, darling?" Les asked, his voice muffled in her hair.

Megan nodded. "Mostly, I didn't want to feel guilty about dragging you away from a life you loved."

"No one is dragging anyone anywhere," Karl said softly against her ear. "During the time we were men, we spent long evenings talking about how things would be once we were mated again."

A bittersweet longing ran beneath his words, and it tugged hard at her heart. With it came the realization that the men may have carved out an existence they could live with, but they'd been lonely. Just like her.

"Exactly," Les said, and she knew he'd been inside her mind.

She glanced skyward. Color had leached from the sunset, and she shivered slightly. The sun had long since dropped below the horizon, taking its warmth along with it. "Thank you." She twisted to look at her mates one at a time.

"For what?" Karl asked.

"Answering me honestly. I guess I needed to hear that this would be a clean slate for all of us. I'm the one with something to run away from. If you two hadn't hooked your star to mine, there'd be no reason for you to leave."

"Oh but you're wrong about that," Les said. "Hunters have become much more aggressive. We killed some recently, and were wondering if getting out of here—even if it meant retreating to the forest as wolves—wouldn't be wiser than staying."

"And that was before Jed called us," Karl added, "and told us things were bad down south too."

"Nothing will truly change," Les muttered, "until we do something about those fucking Hunters—"

Karl shot a meaningful glance at his pack mate. "Not tonight, brother. Tonight, we're going to make love with our new mate.

Tomorrow is soon enough to figure out the Hunter problem. Besides, that discussion has to include Jed. He's our alpha."

"What exactly does that mean?" Megan asked. She ached for her mates, but learning more about her new life was important too.

"We're just like a wolf pack," Les replied. "Jed earned the alpha position by being strong and wise. He fought his way to the top of the pack centuries ago and hasn't faced many challengers."

"What about other kinds of shifters?" she asked.

"They have their own alphas," Karl said. "Bears, coyotes, and mountain cats are the main shifter forms beyond wolves. The four alphas meet from time to time and hammer out policies the rest of us live by."

"Is that enough for right now?" Les pulled her more snuggly into an embrace.

Her crotch flooded and a primal heat swept through her so quickly, she wondered if he'd powered it with shifter magic. Because words felt beyond her, she just nodded. The men flanked her, each with an arm around her, and together they moved into the cabin.

Karl bent and chucked more wood into the stove. Les pushed her into a chair in front of the fire. "You're cold," he observed. "And I've wanted to brush out your hair ever since I first saw it."

"By the time he's done, you'll be warmed up enough to take you to bed," Karl said, kneeling in front of her and unlacing her shoes.

Les stood behind her and tugged pins from her hair while Karl took her feet between his hands, rubbing the cold from them. Once her hair was loose, Les left for a moment, returning with an old boar bristle brush. He worked the stiff, black bristles gently through her tresses, teasing out the tangles.

The more they touched her, even though their caresses weren't specifically sexual, the hotter she became. The merest whisper of her hair against her skin brought her nipples to aching points of need and made her clit throb mercilessly.

Karl ran a nail up the underside of one foot, and then up the other. She pressed her foot into his hands, and they traveled lazily up her calf, tracing the muscles with teasing strokes. Sometimes hard, sometimes soft.

Les let go of the brush and buried his hands in her thick hair, cradling her head between them. "Think of my mouth on your nipples, darling," he murmured. "I'm kissing them, suckling them, biting them. Not hard, but enough to remind you how sensitive they are."

"And imagine my mouth on your nub," Karl went on smoothly. "I have fingers inside you, and I'm tonging your clit, making it grow long and hard like the miniature penis it is."

"You have breasts like a goddess." Les flexed his fingers against her head, then let them trail ever so slowly over her ears and down her neck until his hands rested on her shoulders.

"Close your eyes," Karl instructed. "Feel our magic. Let us make love to you this way first."

She squirmed in the chair. The press of her thighs against each other was almost unbearably sensual and she moaned softly.

"Eyes," Les murmured.

Megan let them drift shut. An electric sensation swirled around her. Not their hands. Their shifter magic. Something that felt like ribbon wrapped her in seductive warmth, pressing against her nipples and moving between her legs. The men's breathing developed a catch, right along with hers.

Throat thick with desire, body so keyed up with wanting release her hips bucked against the chair, Megan waited. This was a different way of making love. The men paid out lust, drawing back before she could tumble into ecstasy, but no one touched her. The only thing stroking her was tiny jolts of pleasure.

Her entire body turned into a screaming mass of nerve endings. Everything spelled sex. Not just her nipples and her clit, but her fingers and toes and eyelids. She held her breath, waiting for where the magic would caress her next, welcoming that stroke, and anticipating the next one.

And then the sensation changed. Fingers, tongues, and cocks added to the magic. She reached for her mates and held them against her as Karl sucked her breasts and Les breathed heat over her swollen nub. That was all it took. Just him breathing on her, and she dissolved into the climax that had been hovering, waiting to be unleashed.

Hot, feral screams filled the cabin. Megan felt shocked when she realized those ungodly shrieks came from her. Her eyes flew open. The men were naked, their cocks at full attention as they worshipped her body.

Karl settled his bottomless dark eyes on her. "Did you enjoy that, sweetheart?"

"Oh my yes. It was strange and hot and amazing all rolled into one."

Les broke into a satisfied grin. "We wanted to give you all the pleasure you could hold."

"We were afraid you'd break and demand a climax, but you trusted us enough to let us walk you along the edge." Karl reached a hand to rub his erection.

Megan finally caught her breath enough that talking wasn't a huge effort. "We still have work to do. You boys need me."

"Well, we need something." Les cocked his head to one side. "What would you like, darling? Would you like one of us to do you while you watch the other one of us jack off?"

Heat rose from her chest, making her even rosier than she figured she must be. She loved watching. Had done a lot of it at the Garden of Eden orgies. There was something about how a man gripped his cock when he was on the edge of coming that mesmerized her.

"I think that's a yes," Karl said and ran his hand up and down his engorged shaft.

Les moved her out of the chair, and sat in it, facing her away from him so she could watch Karl. With firm hands on her hips, he guided her down onto his shaft.

"This is like earlier, but we're all in the same room," she said, glorying in the stretching sensation as Les' cock filled her.

"Mmm-hmm." Karl moved close enough to flick her clit with his other hand. Tugging another chair over, he sat across from her and Les, continuing to stroke himself.

She reached a hand and covered his before he slid out from beneath her, letting her grip his shaft with his hand atop hers. Les rocked into her from behind, and Karl showed her the pressure and motion he needed. Someone tweaked and rolled her nipples. Someone rubbed her clit. It didn't matter whose hands did what. Their mutual arousal kindled and ignited until she was almost as high as she'd been earlier.

Les swelled inside her, and Karl grew larger in her hand. She felt her own peak closing fast, galloping toward her at the speed of light.

"That's right," Les spoke into her mind. *"We're perfectly attuned and we'll all do this together."*

"Higher," Karl urged. *"Hold off, and we'll all go higher."*

Something changed and sensation spilled through her. She felt the heat of her vault around Les and the pressure of her hand around Karl. More shifter magic, but she welcomed it, dove headlong into the lust pummeling her from all directions. Sex thickened the air until she was drowning in lust. When her climax came, it rocked her to her foundations. Les juddered inside her. Karl jerked and spasmed in her hand. She just kept coming until her vision hazed at the edges.

For a long time, the only sound in the cabin was their ragged breathing. Les nuzzled her neck. Karl leaned forward and kissed her mouth before getting up for a towel to wipe his semen off her hand and the floor.

He poured wine into a glass and handed it to her before drinking out of the bottle.

Les held out a hand, and Karl handed the liquor to him.

"Ready to go to bed, darling?" Karl's dark eyes twinkled with joy.

Half a snorting laugh blew past her lips. "I'm not sure I can keep up with the two of you. If bed means sleep, by all means."

"We'll let you sleep. For a while." Les stopped kissing her neck long enough to talk.

"We'll make sure you get all the rest you need," Karl chimed in. "But maybe not tonight. It's been a long time since we had a woman to love."

"You can't blame us for being enthusiastic." Les sent a fond smile her way.

Megan got to her feet and kissed them both. "Not only do I not blame you, I wouldn't have it any other way. Maybe a few minutes of rest before the next round, though?" She furled a brow.

"Whatever you need, love." Karl's expression grew serious.

"What?" she asked.

He shook his head. "Nothing."

"I'm your mate." She gripped his hand. "Tell me what you're thinking. We shouldn't have secrets between us."

"We should take advantage of the moments we have," Les broke in. "No one knows what tomorrow will bring." He pressed his lips into a resolute expression. "Damn it. We'd decided no Hunters. Not in this cabin. Not tonight."

"It's hard to totally block them out," Karl said. "But we'll do our damnedest. Megan deserves all the joy we can provide. She took a huge chance with us, and we owe her everything."

"No. You owe me nothing," she corrected. "From where I sit, you took a chance on a fugitive. To find men to love me and that I love is so incredible I don't have words for it."

"Good place for us to retire to bed, wouldn't you say?" Les looped an arm through one of hers and Karl the other. Leaning into one another, they made their way to the mattresses laid on the floor and cuddled close.

"Sleep, darling," Les murmured.

"Yes, sleep." Karl smoothed hair back from her face. "We'll watch over you."

CHAPTER 11

Dawn was barely breaking when the old farm truck rolled out the driveway and merged onto the road heading for Red Deer. Seated between her mates, Megan laid a hand on each man's leg. They'd decided the night before to get as early a start as possible, and she'd packed them a picnic breakfast to eat en route. A thermos of honey-sweetened tea sat on the floorboards.

"I don't understand why I'm not more tired," she said. "I suppose we got a little sleep, but between talking and making love, we couldn't have gotten much."

"You can lean on one of us and take a nap." Les glanced at her and smiled from his perch behind the wheel.

"That's just it. I'm not tired. I feel more alive and energized than I have—ever."

"It's the shifter magic," Karl said. "We don't need much sleep, and it's looking like that will be one of the things you've absorbed through the mate bond."

Megan reached into a crinkly paper sack and pulled out a bacon and egg sandwich wrapped in waxed paper. She folded back the paper and handed it to Les before fishing Karl's sandwich out of the bag and offering it to him.

"This is great, Megan!" Karl spoke around a mouthful of food, his words slurry.

"I'm glad." The warm glow she'd felt in her midsection ever since meeting her mates cascaded all the way to her toes. She retrieved her own sandwich and took a bite. It was good. The bread, courtesy of Jed, was still fresh and fragrant. The bacon and eggs, also from Jed's largesse, were perfect. Eggs just a bit runny and bacon crisp.

Karl reached for the thermos of tea, unscrewed the cap that doubled as a cup, and poured steaming liquid into it. He blew on it before drinking. A smile split his face. "Sugar's already in it. You think of everything, sweetheart."

She shrugged self-consciously. "Maybe not everything, but I do a fair job in the kitchen. All of us at the orphanage had jobs. Mine was always in the kitchen since I had a flair for taking cheap food and making it edible."

"They didn't feed you well?" Les' voice held a hard edge, as if he wanted to detour past the Calgary orphanage and kill someone.

"There were a lot of us and only so much money to work with. I wasn't usually hungry, but fresh fruits and vegetables were in short supply, unless a local farmer took pity on us. And the meat was mostly tinned. We ate a lot of bread and rice and potatoes."

"I'm so sorry." Karl patted her hand and then draped an arm around her shoulder and pulled her against him.

"Don't be. Other kids had it worse. Lots of homeless youngsters wandered the streets after the flu killed off their families. At least I had a roof over my head." Megan sucked in a quick breath, anxious to change the subject. She didn't want her mates to pity her. "What are we going to do first once we get to Red Deer?"

"Since passports are the big unknown—" Les crumpled the

waxed paper from his sandwich and handed it to her "—we'll begin at the courthouse."

"Excellent idea," Karl seconded. "That way if they have to do some sort of processing, we can come back at the end of the day to pick them up. Shopping shouldn't take all that long."

"Speak for yourself," Megan countered. Karl poured more tea and passed it to her. She drank and offered it to Les. "I need nearly everything, so it will take a couple of hours, even if I hurry."

Les took the tea from her and drained it. "Maybe we'll drop you at one of the ladies' shops then, while we go get another car."

"Will you be keeping the truck?" she asked. Her sandwich had disappeared nearly as fast as the men's. She was still hungry and thinking she should've made two apiece.

"Most likely," Karl answered.

"It might come in handy to have two vehicles. And I can't see how we'd get by without a truck to haul things." Les handed the cup back. "How about another splash?"

Karl refilled the cup. "That's the last of it. Back to our discussion about the cars. I happen to agree with you about keeping the truck. We could drive both of them to the cabin and park the truck in the shed. That way we won't have to decide about it until we return next spring." He paused for a beat. "If we move, the truck will come in really handy."

"So long as that fire doesn't wipe everything out," Les muttered.

The fire.

Smoke had drifted in the treetops like wispy gray ghosts when they left the cabin. Easily visible in the pre-dawn gloom, it hadn't required lupine senses to smell it. "Do you think the fire might really do that?" Anxiety clutched at Megan's belly. Even if she didn't want to live year-round at the cabin, it was still a special place. She'd met her mates there, and it was where they'd first made love.

Hell, it was where I lost my virginity.

"Hard to say," Karl murmured.

"Yeah, it all depends on the wind," Les added, his brow furrowed with worry. "And on how soon the fall rains come."

She passed the empty tea cup back to Karl. For some reason her eyes felt heavy. "Is that offer to lean on you and nap still open?"

"Of course." He tightened his arm around her and drew her against him.

"Good if you can sleep." Les laid a hand on her leg. "No point worrying about the fire. We can't control what it does."

"What about your magic?" she asked sleepily. "Could you use it to keep your cabin safe?"

"That would be useful, but shifter magic has its limitations. Creating shielding that's impervious to fire is one of them. Sleep, love." Les stroked her leg, and her eyes grew heavier.

Megan could barely stay awake. "You did something."

"No," Karl countered. "I did. It's the least I can do for keeping you up most of last night. Sleep, darling. Let yourself drift."

THE FIRST THING she noticed when someone shook her gently awake was the truck wasn't moving. "Are we there?" she asked muzzily.

"Almost," Les said. "We're just to the outskirts of town."

"Yes, we thought you might want to get out and stretch your legs and run a comb through your hair," Karl cut in.

"What time is it?"

"Just closing on nine," Karl answered. "We made good time."

Megan took a quick tally with her sleep-fuzzed brain. Walking around might help clear it. "Gee, I feel like I was drugged."

"That's because you sort of were." Karl massaged her shoulders. "Les wanted to make sure you got a decent rest and so did I. We got to talking, and neither of us realized the other was infusing magic into your sleep spell. Until we tried to wake you."

"So you got a double dose." Les bent toward her and kissed her cheek. "Sorry. It'll wear off fast."

Les opened his door and jumped out. Megan slid behind the wheel and took his hand to help navigate the large step between the running board and the ground. She shook her head and inhaled deeply. It helped, so she did both again. After a quick trip to the thick foliage at the side of the road to relieve herself, her head felt much clearer.

She stepped onto the running board, reached into the cab for her purse, and extracted a comb. Megan had pinned her hair up before they left the cabin. Sections had loosened, so she settled them back into place. "How do I look?"

"Ravishing." Les grinned at her.

"You've got to be the most beautiful woman in the world," Karl said.

Megan felt heat rise from her chest to her face. "Slow down on those compliments. I'll become insufferable."

"Maybe you just need to get used to being appreciated," Karl countered.

She clambered back into the truck. The men followed. Once they were underway, she asked, "If I don't need much sleep, why'd the two of you knock me out?"

"I said you'd need less, not none," Les said.

"Surely I got some sleep last night," she protested. Flashes from the previous evening cavorted through her mind. They'd made love over and over. Each time they fell sated into one another's arms, someone would start up again. Her blush deepened. "Uh, maybe I didn't get as much as I thought."

Karl snorted. "You got more sex than you bargained for and much less sleep."

"Are all newly mated groups like us?"

Les nodded. "Our urges won't settle much for years."

"Alice said something like that," Megan murmured. "But I didn't exactly believe her."

"Do you now?" Karl arched a brow and winked.

"In spades." Megan glanced out the windshield as they moved deeper into Red Deer's downtown area. She recognized the train station. "Where's the courthouse?"

"Only another couple of blocks," Les said. "I'll look for somewhere to park once we're a little closer."

They piled out of the truck. Megan positioned herself between the men, but Les shook his head. "Doesn't look good. Take my arm and Karl will walk behind us."

Megan kicked herself. Of course it didn't look good. The objective was to get in and out of town with what they needed without attracting undue attention that might alert any Hunters who might be nearby. For a moment, she thought about Justin. He'd been on his way to help with the fire, but that was a few days ago. He might've returned.

Let's think positive here. The fire's getting worse. They probably need every able-bodied man they can scare up working the fire line.

She mounted the courthouse steps. They stopped at the building directory to figure out which office handled passports and found it was located one floor up. "Probably good it's the same place it used to be," Les mumbled. "Maybe that means their application procedure hasn't changed, either."

One more flight and Karl pulled a heavy door blazoned with OFFICE OF FOREIGN TRAVEL open. No one else was waiting, so they got the necessary paperwork, clipboards, and pens from the receptionist and settled into folding chairs to fill out the forms. An hour later, they'd been processed and told their passports would be ready for pickup near the end of the day.

"That certainly went smoothly," Karl said once they were outside again.

"Couldn't have been much better," Les agreed. He turned to Megan. "Do you have any idea where you'd like to shop?"

She shook her head. "I've never been here before. I'm sure if we took the truck and cruised through the downtown, we'd find something."

"We can certainly do that." Karl set a brisk pace for the truck. "If it's close to five when the passports are ready, the gather…er…party will be in full swing before we get home."

"I'm not the only one whose brain got addled." Megan flashed a shy smile. "You're a day ahead of yourself."

Karl rolled his eyes. "So I am. The party isn't until tomorrow night."

"Yeah, tonight would've been pushing it." Les stopped for long enough to nudge Karl with an elbow.

Megan let Karl help her into the truck. Once both men flanked her in its cab, she said, "One of you could start home with the truck once you're finished buying the car. That way you'd be there in case Jed arrives earlier than you expected him."

"Good idea." Les patted her leg. "No matter what kind of car we get, the truck will be quite a bit slower. Maybe we'll swing back by the courthouse once we're done with the car and see if they can put a rush on either Karl's or mine."

"What about shopping for the two of you?" Megan asked.

"Probably not all that important. We can always stop at one of the U.S. cities across the border and stock up."

She considered if that strategy would work for her, but she had so little—really, only the clothes on her back—that it wouldn't. So long as she was in shopping mode, she may as well get the lion's share of what she needed. That way she'd be less likely to forget something critical. Besides, it would take the men some time to finish buying a car. The truck rolled to a stop. She glanced out the window. A bank.

"Be right back." Les jumped down. "We need cash."

"Shouldn't be gone more than a few minutes, darling." Karl

exited the other side of the car and then stood on the running board and looked right at her. "Les didn't want me to tell you because he doesn't want you to worry, but there might be Hunters about. It's faint, but we think we scented them. Lock the truck doors and slide down in the seat. If you sense anything at all, scream your head off. We'll hear you."

"Karl." Les' voice rang from the front door of the bank. "Need you in here."

"Less than five minutes." Karl grinned reassuringly before spinning to lope toward Les.

Hunters!

She cranked up the windows, locked the wing windows, and had just locked the doors when the men were back. Her heart pounded and her throat was dry. As soon as Les and Karl were back in the truck, she demanded, "Tell me everything you know about Hunters being close to us."

Les pounded a fist on the steering wheel. "Goddammit, Karl," he sputtered. "We're not even certain ourselves, and you had to get our mate riled up."

"She has a right to know," he said evenly.

"Stop it. I don't want to listen to you argue. I need to know everything you do." Megan twined her hands together in her lap, holding them so tightly her fingers whitened from pressure.

"That's just it," Les said and started the truck's engine. "We know virtually nothing. Karl thought he caught a whiff of Hunter near the courthouse, but it could be vestiges of a scent left a week or a month ago."

"It was faint," Karl admitted. "And I haven't smelled anything since then."

"Regardless," Les said somberly, "the sooner we finish our business here and get moving out of town, the better. Between Karl and me, we'd probably prevail if it came to a direct confrontation, but I'd just as soon not get mired in a pitched battle."

"We never know which side the authorities are going to be on," Karl muttered.

Les clutched the steering wheel so hard, his knuckles made little popping noises. "The hell we don't. It's not going to be ours."

"You're scaring our mate," Karl chided.

"Sorry." Les let go of the wheel and made an expansive gesture. "Look for a shop, Megan. Hunters won't bother you. It's only us they're interested in."

She exhaled sharply, and the smothering sensation in her chest loosened, but not by much. She'd been about to tell her mates she didn't need to shop.

"Sweetheart." Karl leaned into her. "You'll be fine. Hunters have never targeted shifter mates. Take a few deep breaths and enjoy a shopping spree. We'll finish up with the car as fast as we can and meet you."

"If we're really quick about it, maybe we can watch her try things on." Les smirked.

"As if they'd let you in the dressing room with me."

The flash of humor relaxed her. She glanced up and down what looked like Main Street. "Look there." She pointed at three shops in a row that obviously carried women's clothing and necessities. "I should be able to find everything I need at one or the other of those places."

The street wasn't busy, so Les pulled to the curb. Karl got out and then helped her down. He reached into a pocket and placed a wad of folded bills into her hand. "Here's three hundred dollars in twenties. If you need more—"

"Three hundred," she squeaked. "Oh my God, take some of it back. I wasn't planning on spending more than twenty or thirty. Maybe fifty tops."

"Indulge yourself," Les called from behind the wheel. "Buy what you want. If you find something that what we gave you doesn't cover, tell the shop girl to hold it for you, and we'll take care of it once we're back."

Megan blinked back tears. It was hard to swallow around the lump in her throat. "Thank you." She blew Les a kiss and leaned toward Karl.

He shook his head almost imperceptibly. "Have a blast, Sis," he said meaningfully. "What are brothers for?"

CHAPTER 12

Megan strode briskly across the street, tucking the money into her purse as she went. Karl had handed her close to four months' wages as casually as if the sum were insignificant. Her understanding of what her mates meant when they told her money wasn't a problem edged up several notches. Money wasn't much of a problem for her, either, but on a much smaller scale.

She peeked through the windows of each shop and decided which she'd visit first. If she could find most of what she needed in one place, she'd get done that much sooner. She moved from rack to rack of clothing, selecting a few things from each. Always a careful shopper, she tried not to waste time with too many price comparisons. The store filled with patrons as she dipped in and out of the dressing room, adding to her stack of purchases on the clerk's desk each time.

Megan ducked from beneath the curtain shielding her individual dressing room from a larger, common area she assumed the store's seamstress used for fittings. Her arms were laden with skirts, blouses, and sweaters. Before she got to the door leading back into the main part of the store, a hand closed over her arm.

Certain it was a mistake, Megan turned to see who had hold of her. Her eyes widened, and her heart slammed into overdrive. "Justin!" she stammered. "What are you doing back here in the dressing rooms?"

"I'm a cop. I can go anywhere. You seem nervous, Mary. Or was that Megan? Any particular reason?" Blue eyes bored into hers.

"You're about the last person I was expecting to see. It's just a surprise. And I'm scarcely used to men in the ladies' dressing room area." She tried to square her shoulders and pull back, but he held fast.

"A surprise, is it?" His eyes narrowed, and he tightened the hand around her arm. Unlike the night she'd met him, he wore a police uniform. He stood so close his nightstick banged against her hip.

"Let me go. You're hurting me." She yanked her arm, but his grip was like an iron pincer.

The curtain over a dressing room whipped open, and a startled looking woman hurtled out and scurried past them. The same thing happened again. And again.

Justin cocked his head to one side as if he were listening. "It would appear we're alone. Most people scatter once they hear the law's nearby."

Megan's gut clenched. The metallic taste of fear flooded her mouth. She dropped her armload of clothing, doubled her fist, and socked Justin as hard as he could in his side. He grunted and grabbed her other arm. She tried to scream, but her throat was so dry all that came out was a squeak.

"I wouldn't try it, sister," he hissed. "I'm the law. I'd tell whoever showed up you were a hooker, and I was taking you in."

He backed her against a wall and held her with the weight of his body. Positioning her arms over her head, he pinned them easily with one hand and curved the other around her throat.

Fear galloped in, crazy fear thrumming through her body. She writhed against his grasp, tried to knee him in the balls, tried again to shriek for help. He pressed on her windpipe, not hard enough to cut off her air, but her panic spiraled out of control.

"Stop that!" he barked.

More pressure. Spots danced in front of her eyes, and Megan felt herself weaken.

"I'm going to give you a choice," Justin said. "Maybe I'm stupid, but I liked you when I gave you a ride. I knew you were in trouble, but at least you were clean—then." His face was so close to hers, spittle sprayed her face when he spoke. He shook her hard enough her teeth rattled together. "Are you going to stop fighting and listen to me?"

Her head lashed from side to side. "No, I mean yes. Jesus Christ! What the fuck do you want with me?"

A sly expression stole over his features. "Oh, I think you know. I warned you about shifters, and now you've gone and taken up with them. I smell them all over you. Dirty, filthy wench. You're going to lead me to them, so I can do what I was born to do. Rid the planet of their ilk." He drew back a few inches and smiled, actually smiled, at her. "There now, darling. That's not so hard, is it? Just show me where they are, and I'll see you get away from them."

Aw, shit. Shit. Shit. Shit. I can't call for Les or Karl. Got to keep them safe from this madman.

"I—" she choked on snot and started over. "I'm sure I have no idea what you're talking about. I was just shopping for a few winter clothes—"

A sharp slap canted her head to one side. "Don't lie to me, girly. Someone who was thumbing a ride out of here a few days back wouldn't have the funds to *shop for winter clothes*. I'm trying to be nice."

She sneered and drew her lips into a snarl, as anger trumped fear. "What happens when you're not nice?"

"You don't want to know."

Oh yes I do.

Hysteria trod just beneath the surface; she shoved it back where the monsters under the bed live. "I don't know a thing. I can't help you. Now, goddammit, let me go."

"In a pig's eye." he mocked her. "Just remember when you wake up that I gave you a choice."

"What do you mean when I wake up?" His hand on her throat tightened. The other hand let go of her arms. Believing the whole thing was a sick joke and he was finally letting her go, she never saw his other fist, only heard the sickening crunch as it plowed into her jaw. Something heavy clubbed her in the side of the neck. Her head spun wildly just before darkness closed over her.

KARL HEADED FOR THE TRUCK, but Les called him back. "Let's just leave it parked here until we're ready to leave. Makes it easier if we don't have to find parking for two cars downtown."

"Fine." Karl's nostrils flared. "So long as you drive the new one. I do not want to be the one who gets the first scratch on that shiny, dove-gray paint job."

Les slugged him in the arm. "Be that way. Do you think Megan will like it?" He ducked into the low-slung sedan.

"Like it? She'll love it. Let's hurry so we can show it to her." Karl settled into the passenger seat and inhaled noisily. "Wow! Just smell all that leather."

"Better than mouse shit in the pickup, huh?"

"Or the bleach you used to clean it," Karl pointed out and chuckled.

Les backed their brand new Chrysler Imperial Airflow Sedan out of the dealership parking lot and merged into light traffic. They'd traveled about half a mile when it felt like a mule kicked him in the gut.

He whipped his head around. "Did you feel that?"

"Feel what?" Karl looked up from the sales contract he was studying.

"Not sure. It's like someone shit all over my grave."

"You're just nervous because we caught a whiff of Hunter at the courthouse."

Les thought about it. "No. It's more than that. Jesus! I hope Megan's all right."

"She would've called for us if anything went wrong."

"What if she couldn't?"

Karl folded the papers in his hands and placed them in the glove box. "I'd see if I could reach her, but the less shifter magic we deploy, the better off we are. Less visible."

Les nodded his understanding. Every nerve was on edge. He didn't understand why Karl couldn't feel the wrongness. It didn't take long to reach where they'd left Megan. He pulled to the curb in a screech of tires, jumped out of the car, and raced into the first shop with Karl right behind him.

"Help you gentlemen?" A salesgirl with blood red lipstick and nails painted to match simpered.

"I'm looking for my wife." Les tossed his head back. "She's nearly as tall as me with long, blonde hair pulled into a bun. Blue eyes.

The clerk's brows drew together. She bit her lower lip and managed to transfer lipstick to her front teeth. "Haven't seen her. I've been here since we opened. We've only had a handful of customers today. I would have—"

Les didn't wait to hear more. He bolted from the shop. Before he could check out the next one, Karl's hand landed on his shoulder. "Calm down, dammit. You look like a madman. I can almost see your claws and tail."

"Do you finally feel it?" Les demanded.

"Yes. Now we're close I do feel it. This has Hunter stamped all over it." Les tried to shuck Karl's hand, but he wasn't done talking, "I don't think we're going to find her. I don't sense her energy close by. Do you?"

Les drew a shuddery breath and willed himself to stoicism. Karl was absolutely correct—about both things. Megan wasn't in the area, and his wolf was frighteningly close to the surface. He wouldn't be able to help her if he shifted spontaneously and got dragged into a Hunter's net. For all he knew, Hunters had shanghaied Megan and were lying in wait behind some sort of psychic shield.

"That's better," Karl said calmly. He lifted his hand. "Now we can look in the other two shops."

"Do you think it's worth our time since we know she's not here?"

"Yes. We may pick up clues." Karl gave Les a little shove.

It didn't take more than a few moments. The salesgirl in the middle shop remembered seeing Megan and helping her select some clothes, but hadn't seen her leave. She smiled brightly through too much makeup, and her bleached-blonde hair looked like straw. "Sorry, gents. We've had a bunch of women through here this morning. I guess your wife done left when I wasn't paying attention. She accumulated quite a pile of duds on the counter. Would you be wanting to take care of the bill?"

"Maybe we'll just look around a bit," Les said. "We know her size. Maybe we can add to the pile." He and Karl walked to the back of the store. His lupine senses were as fully deployed as possible given the constraints of his human form.

"Do you suppose we could check out the dressing rooms?" Karl sent.

"Not easily. How about if you cover me? I'm sure it's just through that door over there."

"I'll do my best, but if they catch you, there'll be hell to pay."

"Make sure they don't."

Les lingered over a rack of cashmere sweaters until the dressing room door opened and two giggling women emerged, their arms overflowing with clothing. Once the clerk was fully engaged ringing up their purchases at the front of the store, he pulled the door open just enough to slip through and flattened himself against a wall. He sent his magic outward and breathed a sigh of relief once he determined he was alone.

His magic told him far more than that, though. Hunter scent permeated the dressing area, mingled with Megan's. He scented her energy—and her fear. His heart broke for his mate and what she'd faced all by herself, and all because of her connection with him and Les. Rage pummeled him. A claw broke through his index finger.

Les forced himself to take deep breaths as he pushed his wolf side back. No time for that. He listened carefully, determined no one was anywhere near the door except Karl, and slithered back through.

Karl quirked a brow. Les nodded once and trotted toward the front door. The sooner they got out of here, the sooner they could strategize how to get their mate back.

"Sir." The shop girl's voice followed him. "Your wife's clothes."

"Later." Les called over one shoulder and quickened his pace out of the store. Anguish poured through him. Against everything he'd ever believed, Hunters had taken their mate. When the fuck had those bastards begun targeting women?

He turned to Karl to tell him what he'd found, but his pack mate forestalled him. "I already know. I see it in your mind. Back to the car." Karl hooked an arm through his and practically dragged Les to the Chrysler. "Get us somewhere we're not so visible. This car sticks out like a sore thumb. We need to park it and go on foot."

"We've got to locate Jed." Les gunned the engine and drove toward the edge of town.

"Yes, we need him, but that's downstream. Maybe we could track Alice. I'm betting there's a back way out of that store."

Les clenched his jaw so hard, he was surprised his teeth didn't crack. He drove a few blocks to a more wooded area and parked the car. The Chrysler was still flashy and noticeable, but he couldn't do anything about it. Karl slammed his door and reached for the key to lock it. The men didn't need to talk. They'd hunted together for years as wolves and as men.

Les tipped his head slightly. Karl nodded and they took off at a brisk trot for the alleyway that had to run behind the dress shops. Les' nose twitched. Thank Christ Karl had maintained a cool enough head to think of doing this. Hunter scent was strong in the alley, along with their mate's.

Les aimed for a casual air as they followed the scent track. More interested in making certain not to lose the trail than in his surroundings, he turned hard right and would've kept going, but Karl hissed, *"Stop!"* into his mind.

"Why? We're almost—" Les glanced up and froze. He was on the front walkway leading to the local constabulary building. Confusion rocked him, and he stood rooted in place.

Karl beckoned from back on the street. His voice rang with false cheer. "Courthouse is next door. You're not paying attention —as usual. Come on."

"Of course." Les scratched his head and did an about face. "Stupid of me." Because he was practically certain someone might be watching them, Les led the way to the courthouse. He'd wondered why the Hunter hadn't even tried to mask his track. Now he knew. Megan was obviously in jail with no easy way to get to her.

They were in and out of the courthouse in less than ten minutes with all three passports in hand. The receptionist had wagged a finger at them and said she wasn't supposed to hand over official documents to anyone other than the one whose name was on them, but Les cast a mild compulsion spell, and she'd smiled and passed Megan's to him.

"Back to the car," Les sent.

"Agreed. We need to find Jed and the others. I fear this will escalate into an all-out war before we're done."

They covered the few blocks to the Chrysler in silence. Les

balled his hands into such tight fists that they ached. Once he got behind the wheel and Karl was seated, he started the engine and headed for the outskirts of town. They had kin not far from Red Deer. If they couldn't find Jed…

"At least we know it's a cop that nabbed her." Venom made Karl's voice harsh. "A fucking cop."

"No wonder he had carte blanche in the ladies' dressing rooms," Les snarled. "Ach, poor Megan. I swear, if she's been injured in any way, I'll tear that bastard who took her limb from limb."

"And any other Hunter who crosses our path. Maybe they were onto something at the last gathering. We need to kill every single one of those scum-sucking abominations."

"Funny." Les smacked a fist on the steering wheel. "That's what they call us."

"Well, when we say it, it's true. We come from proud stock. Ancient stock. Hunters are newly hatched. They have no rights here."

"Tell them that." Les thought about Megan and how scared she must be and felt ill.

"Try to raise Jed," Karl suggested. "He was supposed to be in town today too."

"Right. I'd forgotten that. I need to be outside this car, though. All the metal will interfere with telepathic transmission." Les spied a dirt track overhung with lush willows, pulled the car beneath a tree, and parked. Out in a trice, he sent his mind voice howling across all the distance he could muster.

"What?" Jed answered almost instantly. *"Calm down."*

"No way. Hunters have Megan."

"They nabbed her at least an hour ago, maybe longer," Karl cut in, obviously having tuned into Les' telepathic channel.

"Son of a bitch. Where are the two of you?"

"On the western edge of Red Deer just off the main highway," Les answered.

"Stay put. We're on our way. I'll raise the alarm and get all of us I can to help."

"Pull out all the stops," Les shouted. Fury tightened his muscles, and a red haze swam before his eyes. *"Call out the bears and coyotes and mountain cats."*

"Maybe you should leave Alice somewhere safe," Karl ventured.

"No way in hell," Alice snapped, her voice resolute through their mind link. *"Megan's in trouble. I want to help."*

CHAPTER 13

Megan sat on a hard bench in the women's drunk tank in the Red Deer jail. Justin had dumped her there hours ago. Her neck ached, and she rubbed gingerly at her swollen jaw. More to have something to do than anything else, she tugged the pins from her hair and braided it to get it out of the way.

Three Indian women sat scattered about the small room. One was quite old, with long, white braids. So far no one had said a word to her. She'd pleaded with the desk sergeant who booked her that she wasn't drunk, but he exchanged glances with Justin and said, "Officer McCollum is one of our best. Keep your mouth shut, Missy, and you'll get out of here sooner."

"I'll take care of her," Justin had said with a grim smile. "I'll see she gets back home tomorrow. Maybe this will teach her to keep her beak out of the hooch."

Megan rolled his words around in her mind. He'd said them for a reason: to let her know he was in control and that she was far from done with him.

What a travesty. I can't complain about him. No one would believe me since I'm a prisoner now and he's a cop.

She wrapped her arms around herself and rocked back and forth. Tears squeezed from the corners of her eyes. She only had a few hours, and Justin would haul her out of this cell and take her God-only-knew where.

I only hope I'm strong enough to protect my mates from discovery. Alice said Hunters could see into my mind. I've got to discover a way to keep Justin out.

An unpleasant thought intruded. Justin was probably preparing somewhere to sequester her, maybe even to torture her. If it had been ready, she'd already be there. Unable to sit still, she jumped to her feet and paced from one side of the cell to the other. She had to get out of there. Had to. Or else find a way to kill herself. Once Justin came for her, she'd be as good as dead anyway.

"Give it a rest," one of the Indians said. A youngish woman, she was full-figured with a beak of a nose and stringy black hair. "They gotta let you out in twenty-four hours. Then you can find another bottle."

"I'm not a drunk," Megan sputtered.

The woman snorted and tossed her head. "Yeah, right. Don't get your knickers in a bunch, hon. It's just us chickens here."

The wraith-thin older woman got to her feet and drew her white brows together into a single line low on her forehead. She stalked toward Megan and came to a halt directly in front of her. "I am Julaika."

"Er, Megan. Nice to meet you." She extended a hand out of habit. Julaika just stared at it, so Megan dropped it to her side.

The woman bent close, nostrils flaring. Her features mirrored surprise for a brief moment before her impassive expression returned. Julaika jerked her head to one side. "Over here, white woman." She strode to the curtained alcove that held a sink and toilets and stepped behind the curtain.

"Why?" Megan stayed put. She needed to find a way out of her dilemma, not indulge a drunken Indian. Although, while the other two women reeked of cheap gin, Julaika smelled of earth and herbs.

The old woman's wizened bronze face and braids appeared to one side of the curtain. "It is white man's curse to always have to know everything in advance. You have nowhere to go. Nothing else to do. If you don't like what I have to say, you can always resume pacing." Julaika cackled and ducked back behind the faded plaid curtain. Megan wondered if she was crazy. Maybe this was the only holding area for women and all of them—drunks, thieves, the mentally unbalanced, murderers—ended up here until they could be transferred elsewhere.

Megan bit her lip hard. Pain had a settling effect. Julaika was right. She didn't have anything better to do, so she sucked in a breath and covered the ten feet between where she stood and the curtain separating the bathroom from the rest of the cell. Another breath and she pulled the curtain aside. Julaika had dropped the lid on one of the two commodes and sat, legs crossed, deeply-veined hands folded in her lap.

Megan looked at the second toilet. It didn't have a lid, but she sat on it anyway—and waited. Minutes ticked past. "Well?" Megan extended her hands, palms up.

The corners of Julaika's mouth twitched. "Another white man's problem, impatience."

"Look. If you're planning to lecture me about all our short-comings, I'm going back out there." She waved a hand at the curtain. "It smells better."

"You can hear me this way. Don't deny it."

Megan drew back. Her mouth fell open before she got hold of herself and snapped it shut. Not much point in denial since her face and actions gave her away, so she nodded bleakly.

"I know McCollum. And I smell him on you. He is bad news for our kind. One of our relatives will come for Trina soon. I can cast illusion so you look like her."

"I-I'm not very good at this." Megan's mind voice was small and

tentative. She wanted to ask hundreds of questions. Like was Julaika a shifter mate? And why was she in jail? But those things weren't important. *"Which one is Trina? Won't she mind if I leave in her stead?"*

Julaika snorted. *"The younger, thinner woman. Of course she'll mind, but she is my sister's daughter-in-law and will obey me. We will give you three hours, and then she'll raise hell about spirits and demons. White men will chalk it up to her being crazy because of hooch."*

Suspicion knifed into Megan. Things were bad, but impersonating another prisoner could make them much worse. *"I don't see how you can pull this off. I'm blonde and about six inches taller than her. Plus, why would you do this for me?"*

"You're Les and Karl's mate. I can smell them all over you too. They've been a great help to my people, the Cree. When winters are bad, they hunt for us as wolves and leave us meat. We used to have shifters of our own to hunt, but not anymore."

Megan took a chance. *"For you to have magic, you must be mated to shifters."*

The old woman's face screwed up in pain. She pressed her lips into a hard line. *"I am, or I used to be. McCollum got both my mates and my brother too."*

"I'm sorry." Megan spoke out loud and laid a hand over Julaika's.

"Bastards," she hissed. "White bastards. I'd kill every last one of them if I could."

Megan knew what she meant. Anger burned hot inside her, curdling her gut. She bent toward Julaika and kissed her cheek. "I hate them too. Why are you here?"

The old woman rolled her eyes. "They think I'm crazy. I threw a rock at one of the police station windows, but I did it to get inside." Her mouth pursed into a grimace. "I needed to check on my Trini. She drank so much she was passed out when they hauled her in here, and I was worried about her."

"That was very kind of—"

Julaika waved her to silence. "Bullshit. I wanted to make certain no one raped her while she was unconscious. They'll let me out in a few hours. They don't have sovereignty over the Cree. Eventually, they have to turn me and the other women over to the Tribal Council."

"What will the council do?"

Julaika's lips drew back, lending her a feral look. "Nothing. We indulge white men. Someday we will take our lands back."

Megan switched back to telepathic speech. *"Who's coming for Trina?"*

"One of our cousins. I will let her know ahead of time about what we're doing."

"How?"

Julaika grinned. *"Why, the same way you and I are talking. Relax. You'll feel my spell around you. When the time comes, embrace it."*

Megan blew out a breath. Julaika's magic must be strong, much more than she expected to absorb from her mates through the shifter bond. The old woman nodded, as if she'd read Megan's thoughts. "I am medicine woman for the Cree. The two magics give me more power than either alone."

"Synergistic," Megan murmured. Julaika tilted her head, a question in her eyes, but Megan said, "It doesn't matter. Another bad white man trait. Over explaining with big words."

A warm smile lit the old Indian woman's face. "Maybe there is hope for you yet. I will work out what must be done with Trina and our cousin, Sara. Go sit on your bench. Trina will sit next to you. When the cell door opens, get up like you have every right in the world to leave. Don't dawdle. As soon as you're well clear of the station, open your mind so your mates can find you."

"What if McCollum's out there?"

"He will not see you so long as you're in the station. Once you are outside, you'll have to find cover." Julaika gave her a little shove. "Get moving. There's not much time."

Megan trotted to the bench she'd been sitting on and forced

herself to sit. Her heart beat so fast, she thought she might faint. Sweat beaded her forehead and upper lip and dripped down her sides. She inhaled deeply, held it, and blew it out. Then she did it again. Julaika's magic might be potent, but Megan still had to play her part. Right now, her legs shook so badly, she wasn't certain they'd hold her upright, let alone allow her to march out the door with her head high.

The bench creaked as Trina sat right next to her, so close the sides of their bodies touched. Megan opened her mouth to thank the other woman, but she turned deep, dark eyes on Megan and shook her head slightly. Trina gathered her long, black hair and quickly tucked it into a bun so it matched Megan's.

Julaika sidled over and laid a hand on each of them for the briefest of moments. A jolt of dizzyingly strong magic shot through Megan. She caught her breath, awed by its raw power. It shimmied around her and Trina like a live thing. Megan struggled to embrace the spell as Julaika had instructed. It felt like trying to hang onto lightning. With a knowing smile, Julaika moved to the far side of the room and perched on a bench facing them.

Trina giggled. "The old one is stronger than she looks, eh?" She lowered her voice. "Sara is almost here. Get ready."

Keys clanked in the metal lock just before the cell door sprang open. A tall, imperious woman with a blue and green blanket wrapped around her and a long, black skirt stood in the doorway. "Get moving, goddammit," she growled. "You bring shame on our people every fucking time I have to bail you out of this place."

Trina gave Megan a little shove. She rocketed to her feet and loped toward Sara. "I'm sorry, cousin. Truly, I am. I'll stay away from the hooch. Promise."

Sara draped an arm around her. "I'll hold you to it. Here's your purse. Desk sergeant didn't want to give it to me, but I insisted. Now get moving. I had a busy afternoon. This wasn't on my schedule."

Megan leaned into Sara and let the other woman lead her

down a long linoleum hallway and past the booking desk where McCollum and the desk sergeant sat with their heads together. She caught a glimpse of them out of the corners of her eyes. Fear cut deep and she would have slowed, but Sara pinched her shoulder hard and towed her along. "Told you," she snapped. "We have to hurry. I'm late for the sweat lodge ceremony."

"Of course. Sorry." Megan matched Sara's pace. In moments, they marched through the front door and out into late afternoon daylight.

Megan started to pull away, but Sara said, "Not yet," and led her several blocks from the stationhouse before finally loosening her hold. "There. I think we pulled it off." Sara stepped back. "Do you want to come to the reservation?"

"Probably not. I don't want to get any of you in trouble. Thanks for getting my purse out of there. How'd you get them to give it to you? I'd have thought they'd have given you Trina's."

"Illusion. Julaika's not the only one with magic. Now about the reservation—"

"I couldn't bother you further. You saved my life as it is."

"Nonsense. Les and Karl are like family. Come on. The magic there will shield you."

"Do you think it's safe for me to call for my mates?"

"It'd be safer if you were on Cree land."

Megan nodded. The reality that she'd really and truly escaped was just setting in. Adrenaline thrummed through her, and she felt like doing a victory dance. "How far?"

"A mile. We can be there in fifteen minutes if you hurry."

"I'm game."

She broke into a trot. Sara paced her. Megan wondered what Les and Karl were doing. If she was any judge, they'd found Jed, and everyone would be trying to free her. Truth in her thoughts slapped her in the face, and she forced herself to move faster.

Sara panted next to her, and her own breath burned in her lungs. Safety was close enough to taste, but would they make it before Justin realized he'd been duped and raced after them in a car? He'd figure out quick enough where they were headed.

Sara slowed, sucking air like a bellows. "All right. We just passed through the boundary to Cree land."

Megan glanced around her, but didn't see anything different. "Are you sure? How do you know?"

A corner of Sara's mouth turned downward. "I can feel it, white woman. Call your mates."

Megan threw her mind wide open. In seconds Karl and Les' voices pummeled her. Where was she? Was she safe? Megan thought she heard Jed and Alice in the background. *Yes, I'm all right. I'm—"* she cast a glance at Sara, who'd probably eavesdropped on her question.

"We're on the southern border of Cree lands between Dancing Deer and Singing Horse streets."

Megan relayed the information along with a ten second version of how she'd escaped from the jail.

"Aw, Jesus." Les sounded near tears—and furious enough to kill Justin. *"We'll be there very soon."*

"Sooner than soon," Karl seconded. The connection faded.

Sara grinned.

"You could hear them, right?" Megan asked.

"Of course. I was mated to Julaika's brother and another shifter clan mate."

Megan remembered what the old woman had told her about Hunters having gotten them. "I'm so sorry."

"I don't think they're dead. I'd feel it here—" Sara tapped her breast bone "—if they were. McCollum and the Hunters, they do something with shifters. Imprison them and suck their magic. It's how they're able to sniff out shifters."

"Do you think Julaika's mates are still alive too?"

Sara nodded. "Someday, we'll be strong enough to find where they are and free them."

"Jed's here. Maybe he can help with that."

The stern look on Sara's face softened. "Head of the wolf shifter clan?" Megan nodded. "Humph. Maybe he can. My mates have been gone so long, I've been afraid to let myself hope. More and more, it's a white man's world. Even if I wasn't mated to shifters, no one cares about a squaw's missing husband."

Thick foliage off to Megan's left rustled menacingly. For one long, heart-stopping moment, she imagined Justin and his cronies leaping out at them. She cast wildly about, but there wasn't anywhere to hide that didn't involve moving right toward where the crash of branches was getting louder. She pivoted, intent on flight, but Sara caught her arm.

"You called your mates." Sara pulled her blanket more firmly around her. "They're nearly here."

Wolves, two coyotes, a mountain cat, and a bear dashed from the forest. In a twinkling, the two in the lead shimmered into men. Karl raced to Megan and scooped her into his arms. Les embraced both of them, pushing his way into their shared hug. Everyone was laughing and crying all at the same time. Relief to find her mates unharmed made Megan's knees weak and brought a lump to her throat. Her eyes flooded with tears.

"I was so afraid you'd try to get me out of jail," she snuffled. "And that McCollum would get you and send you to wherever Sara's and Julaika's mates are."

Jed strode forward, Alice by his side. She tried to push clothes into his arms, but he shook his head. "There are more important things than me being naked." He inclined his head toward Sara. "Sister. I heard some of your conversation with Megan. Do you have any idea where your mates are being held?"

"No. Julaika has more magic than any of us, and even she can't find them."

"How long have Hunters held them?" Bron crowded close.

Sara looked skyward. "It will be a year at the next full moonrise."

Jed exchanged a glance with Bron. His lieutenant nodded

grimly. "I can salvage them, but only if we find them quickly. Once a year has passed, my healing magic has less effect."

Megan gazed around the clearing and counted ten men, all shifters. Besides Jed, Terin, Bron, and her own mates, there were five others she'd never met before.

Jed stood tall and faced the men. "I'd like to find our Indian clan mates. What do the rest of you want to do? We live by democratic rule."

"We're in," Bron and Terin said with one voice.

Les kissed one of Megan's cheeks, Karl the other. "We have to do this," Les told her. "Go with Sara. You'll be safe on the reservation. McCollum and the others can't enter tribal lands."

"Yes," Karl seconded, his arms still tight around her. "I'm so glad to see you, I'm beside myself, but maybe if we fight back harder, they'll think twice about waging war on us."

Megan started to protest but swallowed the words. She wanted to leave this place with her mates right now and never look back, but Julaika and Sara were the reason she was free. If there was a way to release their mates from Justin and his Hunter cronies, she wouldn't stand in the way.

"I'll help," one of the strange men cried out. The others chorused, "Me too."

"Great." Jed rubbed his hands together. Fire blazed from his blue eyes. "It's a clean sweep. Animal forms, men. We're going to do a little hunting of our own."

"I love you." Megan kissed first Les and then Karl.

"And we love you," they told her, kissing her back.

"Soon," Les promised. "We'll make up for being separated."

Karl brushed his knuckles over her lips. "That's a guarantee, love." He jogged toward Jed, with Les right behind him.

Alice walked to Megan and Sara. "Looks like I'm going with you. The car is close. I was tracking the pack with it. Give me a few minutes to round it up, and we'll drive wherever Sara wants us to go on the reservation."

"Great." Megan hugged her. "Waiting is hard. It will be good to have company."

Sara inclined her head and held out a hand to Alice. "It is good to meet another shifter mate. Gives me hope we will not die out."

Alice pumped her hand. "No one is dying out on my watch." She smiled grimly. "Back in a flash with the car."

CHAPTER 14

*L*es reached for his wolf form and joined the pack. They edged deep into the woods they'd emerged from a few moments before. There would've been more of them, but he hadn't wanted to wait for Jed to summon anyone else. Neither had Karl. They'd been frantic about getting to Megan before the Hunter moved her somewhere. As it was, it had taken Jed nearly an hour to gather the other five shifters and join up with them on the outskirts of town.

Jed's voice sounded in his mind, asking for ideas from all of them.

Karl answered. *"Pull up in that grove of fir trees. Les and I spent weeks trying to find those five Indian shifters right after they disappeared."*

Yeah, Les thought. *And that was when their trail was fresh.*

He was still amazed—and deeply grateful—that Megan managed to free herself. What a stroke of luck the old medicine woman had been in her cell. He bent his haunches beneath him, dug in his front claws, and skidded to a halt. At Jed's signal, he found his human form along with the other men. It was easier to talk and plan that way.

"I wanted to get us away from the women," Jed said gruffly. He turned to Les and Karl. "Fill us in on where you looked for our missing clan brothers."

After listening for a bit, Jed shook his head. "Crap! You were thorough, and it doesn't bode well. Tell us where you didn't look."

"That's just it." Les frowned. "At the time, we thought we looked everywhere."

"We were really methodical about it," Karl chimed in.

"Sounds to me like the Hunters were onto you and moved our kin every time you got close," the bear shifter grumbled.

"If that's true," Les countered, "why didn't they ever try to capture us?"

"They probably had their hands full with the five they shanghaied," Terin muttered.

"Sounds about right," Bron agreed. "It was bold of them to take so many of us, and much too risky to leave our brothers in one place."

Jed snapped his fingers. "That's it. They separated them, which means our pack brothers have to be close to town. It would take too much time to keep more than one location secure if the Hunters had to travel any distance."

"But we checked everywhere." Karl threw his hands into the air.

"Yes." Les narrowed his eyes. "We did check everywhere—once. And even a few places that smelled promising more than that. What if our bear brother is right and the Hunters simply moved their captives to a location we'd just visited? Staying one step ahead of us."

"Makes sense." Jed clamped his jaws together so hard his teeth clacked against each other. "How does this sound? We wait till dark, since it won't be long now, and take our animal forms. We'll split into five groups. One group will begin at the north end of town, one at the south—"

"We'll take east and west." The coyote, bear, and mountain cat shifters spoke over one another. "We're used to hunting together."

"I'll take south," Terin said. He walked to the sixth wolf shifter. "Will you accompany me, brother?"

"Of course."

"Karl and I will take north," Les said.

"Excellent," Jed went on. "Bron and I will begin in the center of Red Deer and fan outward in circles. If anyone finds something promising, he can alert the rest of us."

"What exactly are we looking for?" Karl asked. "How many locations?"

"There have to be at least two, and we will not move on either until we've located both."

"You're afraid once we show our hand, the Hunters will go all out to protect whichever place we're not at," the coyote shifter muttered.

Jed shrugged. "It's what I'd do. Standard warfare tactics."

"Maybe we could begin our reconnaissance in human form before we lose the light," Les suggested. "From what Megan said, the Hunters will be frantic to find her once they discover what happened at the jail. It might divert their attention from what we're doing."

"Risky," Karl noted. "But a good idea. I'm afraid at least that one Hunter, McCollum, knows what Les and I look like. It must've been his scent we caught at the courthouse when we were filling out the paperwork for our passports. I'll bet he trailed us from there to where we let Megan off."

"He's probably known about us since we tried to find those Indian shifters," Les gritted through clenched teeth. "Bastard! No matter what happens today, he's a dead man. I'll track him from here to Newfoundland if I have to."

"Know how you feel, bro—" Karl jabbed him with an elbow "—but our mate would miss you."

"Enough." Jed clapped his hands together. "Let's get moving.

Report only if you find something. We want to use as little magic as possible. No point in alerting those nasty ass sons of bitches to our presence any sooner than we have to."

~

LES CREPT from shadow to shadow, restless in his wolf form. His sensitive lupine nose examined one scent after another, seeking elusive clues. Karl's energy pulsed off to one side. They'd been at it for hours, and the moon was well on its transit across the sky. He glanced about. They were nearing the center of town. The streets were deserted, but it was still dangerous to remain in a place with so little cover as a wolf. He couldn't shift. His clothes were back by the Chrysler on the far side of town. Being naked was one step up from being a wolf, but only a small one.

He was just about to join Karl and suggest they call it a night and rejoin their mate when something tickled his nostrils. He tilted his head back and shut his eyes, inhaling deeply.

Yes.

Something odd. Something that shouldn't be there, bounced sourly between his shifter magic and the scent receptors in his nose.

Karl bumped his flank. Les exchanged glances with him, understanding he'd smelled it too. They turned as a unit, muzzles raised, and padded silently toward the subtle alteration that had alerted Les in the first place. As they got closer, the stink of Hunter magic formed and intensified. Yet there was something beneath it too. Something Hunters had gone to a great deal of trouble to mask with spells.

"We should call Jed." Karl's voice brushed the surface of Les' mind, and he remembered they were to do nothing until they'd found both sites.

"We need more information. What if Jed's wrong and they're all here?"

"*Agreed on more information, but Jed's orders were specific,*" Karl reminded him.

Les jerked his muzzle down in agreement. His pack mate was right. Jed was their alpha and they obeyed his directives. It was what kept the pack healthy. Withdrawing to the lee side of a ratty shed, he ducked inside. Karl followed and pulled an invisibility spell about them that would partially mask their presence—and conversation. They needed to discuss what happened next.

"*Something's in the basement of that big, white house across from where we stopped.*" Hope speared through Les, followed by a hefty shot of adrenaline. "*Maybe it's our brothers.*"

"*We didn't exactly smell them.*"

"*Close enough. Whatever's down there has Hunter stamped all over it, and why would they go to so much trouble to hide anything but imprisoned shifters?*"

"*Who knows what other secrets Hunters have?*" Karl muttered.

Les thought about it. "*Not sure about secrets, but the location seems too close to town.*"

"*What better place to hide something than in plain view? It's what Jed would call warcraft. I say we alert the pack.*"

"*Agreed.*" Les extended his mind-voice to reach Jed and the others.

"*Any other hits?*" Jed asked the pack. When no one responded, he went on. "*Work your way slowly toward—*"

"*I've got something.*" The coyote sounded excited. "*After listening to Les' description, I realized we passed the same thing a while back.*"

"*Yes,*" the bear broke in with his deep, rumbly voice. "*We circled back to it while you were talking, and it's a definite hit.*"

"*Your position?*" Jed barked. Once he heard, he deployed the nearest pair, which happened to be the mountain cats, to join the coyote and the bear. His parting shot was, "*Kill those motherfuckers who kidnapped our kinfolk.*"

"*We intend to,*" the bear shot back.

"*Listen up.*" Jed's command voice rang in Les' head and presumably everyone else's as well. *"Get in and out. Springing our kin is our first priority. If we can do that without laying hands on any Hunters, so much the better."*

"But you told us to kill them," the coyote protested.

"Only if you have to. I've rethought things. It's in our best interest to remain invisible."

"Shit!" the bear grumbled just before falling silent.

Les ground his wolf jaws together. He wanted to kill, but the rational part of him understood Jed's logic. The less damage they did, the better. After all, Hunters could complain to the authorities that they'd imprisoned shifters and the shifters in question had escaped. By comparison, shifters had zip squat in the way of rights. If they were caught killing humans, they'd be shot or hung.

Jed and the other wolves joined him and Karl. They loped toward the big, white house at the end of a dark street, slowing once they grew close. Jed nosed a basement window and then padded around the house, returning to the tight knot they'd formed at the edge of a manicured lawn. The air around him shimmered as he reached for his human form.

"The rest of us?" Les sent.

"No. I need fingers to break in. Stand ready, Bron. I may need you human for a quick jolt of healing energy. Goddess only knows what we'll find inside."

The window latch rattled, sounding loud to Les' sensitive ears. Jed pulled it open and jimmied his body inside. A sharp intake of breath and then, *"Holy fucking Christ!"*

Karl shot past Les and leapt into the blackness beyond the window. Les followed. The first thing that hit him once he passed wards that were obviously entwined with the house walls, was the smell. Shit, vomit, rotten food. Three of the Indian shifters they'd hunted for so long sat in their own filth in cages so small they were hunched forward, locked into squatting positions. Les looked closer and recognized Julaika's mates and her brother. They were still alive, barely.

Horror filled him, along with fury. Les pushed both aside. Emotions were an indulgence. Now wasn't the time for them.

He made a grab for his human form and started on one of the locks as soon as he had fingers. He spun the padlock, listening intently for its tumblers. In moments, one cage was open. He started on another while Jed, Terin, and Karl, back in human form as well, dragged the comatose shifter out and onto his feet. The man groaned piteously while they half dragged him across the dirt-floored basement and boosted him up and through the open window.

The sixth wolf shifter padded around the basement, growling until Jed swatted his rump and sent him outside to help care for the sick men.

Jed called for Bron, instructing him to do his best.

"Got it, boss. I'll take it from here. How many more?"

"Two."

"Send Terin out. He can help revive the others while I work on this one."

"I'll help too," the sixth shifter growled. *"Bastards. Fuckers. I'd like to stuff them into those pens. Right after I cut their balls off."*

They'd just helped the third captive shifter outside into Terin's waiting arms when lights flashed on in the basement. Les and Karl spun, hands raised to call power.

"Goddammit," Jed swore as he joined them. "I was hoping we wouldn't have to do this." He sent magic spinning toward the bulbs suspended from the ceiling. Both shattered, giving them the advantage of darkness once again.

Heavy footsteps sounded on the stairs. Les listened intently. Only one man. He hoped it was McCollum. He wanted the bastard to pay for kidnapping Megan—and for what Hunters had done to the Indians they'd held captive. *"Wolves?"*

"What else?" Karl's war whoop rang in his mind as he shifted.

As one, they rushed toward the stairwell with Jed right behind them. The man had to be McCollum. His scent matched what Les had smelled in the shop's dressing room where Megan had disappeared.

A shotgun blast nearly deafened him, but the pellets didn't hit any of them. Les had had enough. The combination of Megan's hell plus the caged shifters raged through him. He lunged up the stairs, fastened his jaws around the man's ankle and pulled hard.

The Hunter tumbled to the bottom. Karl leapt on him, followed by Jed and Les.

"*Quick kill,*" Jed shouted. "*And then we're gone.*"

Karl sank his teeth into a carotid on one side, Les took the jugular on the other. Jed demolished the femoral arteries. Blood geysered everywhere. "*Enough.*" Jed raced for the open window. Les only paused long enough to take in the Hunter's uniformed body, tossing in death throes. McCollum was stamped on one pocket.

Yes! Triumph surged through Les. *I was right about his scent. We got him. I can't wait to tell Megan.*

Les cleared the window sill in a single leap and followed his pack into the night. They hadn't gone far. The three captives were in terrible shape. Bron knelt over them in human form, chanting.

"*Got to get them back to the reservation.*" Jed pivoted in a circle, still in wolf form. "*Which way is it?*"

"*Couple of miles,*" Les replied.

"*Too far. They'll never make it,*" Terin muttered.

"*I'm amazed that shotgun didn't bring half the neighborhood running,*" Karl said.

"*They probably couldn't hear it.*" Les' tail swished from side to side. "*Just like the place was warded to keep smell in, it likely muted sound too, or our pack mates' screams might've alerted someone.*"

"*Good point,*" the sixth shifter muttered. "*I don't live that far from here, and I never guessed. Feeling pretty ashamed of myself.*"

Jed paced from one Indian to the next, nosing, licking, whining encouragement. "*We didn't get this far only to fail.*"

Bron looked up from the painfully thin shifters. He didn't waste magic on telepathy. "I'm trying."

"Just keep 'em alive," Jed snapped. *"I have an idea. It's a risk, but our existence is at stake. We have to get out of here before someone finds that body."*

"It was McCollum," Les snarled.

Jed rounded on him. *"I'm glad he's dead—for your sake—but killing a law officer carries stiff penalties."*

"I don't give a shit. Given a choice, I'd do it again."

"Me too," Karl muttered.

For a few minutes, everyone helped Bron with his spells. The healer was obviously tiring faster than the captives were stabilizing. Headlights pierced the darkness. Jed bounded toward the approaching car, morphing to human midstride.

Les called him back. When that didn't work, he loped after Jed, thinking their clan leader had lost his mind. And then he recognized the car and saw Alice behind the wheel. So that was the risk Jed alluded to. Brilliant! He must've raised Alice and told her to bring the car around for transport. Human in an instant, Les raced to the feeble shifters. Working in teams, they ferried the sick men to the back seat of Alice's car. As soon as they were done, Jed reached through the window and squeezed his mate's shoulder. "Get going. Roll up the window. Don't stop for anyone. If they're standing in front of you, drive over them."

"Aren't you coming?" She clutched his hand.

Reflected in moonlight, Jed's blue eyes looked flat and hard. "No. Got to help the others. There are two more. Once you've dropped these off, wait for my call. I'm guessing our other brothers won't be in any better shape."

Megan worked side-by-side with Sara and two other Indian women boiling water, cleaning abscessed skin, and bathing the emaciated shifters. She'd been reduced to tears of relief when Alice reassured her that she'd laid eyes on Les and Karl and both were all right, but that had been hours ago. Sometime during the long night, Sara had treated her bruises with a poultice of leaves. It reduced the swelling, but her neck and jaw were still sore.

Dawn lightened the windows of the sweat lodge where they'd taken the men. Rain drummed heavily on its tin roof. Shortly after they'd gotten to the lodge the previous afternoon, the skies had opened. At least it meant the fires burning to the west were likely on their way to being extinguished, and her mates' cabin was safe.

The buffalo hides covering the door rustled. Bells sewn into them tinkled discordantly. So many people had come and gone, Megan didn't even look up from the man she worked over. A volley of Cree, as discordant as the bells, blasted her, followed by a high-pitched shriek.

"Oh, for the love of Pete." Megan pushed to her feet, turned, and ran right into Julaika. Tears streamed down the old woman's face as she threw her body over the man Megan had been working on. In between hugging and kissing him, the old medicine woman stood so she could embrace Megan.

"Thank you. By our peoples' god, Kice Manito, I thank you." She beamed through her tears. "Even after I knew what you were, I hesitated before I offered to help you, but the Atayohkanak, er, spirits told me I was wrong to withhold my aid." Her gaze wandered to a man who was struggling to sit.

Megan intuited it had to be her other mate. "Go." She gave Julaika a little push. "We'll have time to talk once you've been reunited."

Speaking of which… Megan straightened her back and rotated both shoulder blades. She'd been hunched over one man or another for a long time. The Indian women seemed to have everything under control. When she looked for Alice, she found the other woman dozing in a corner, head propped on her hand.

Megan was just looking for a spot she could settle and close her eyes for a few moments when the bell-laden buffalo hides chimed again. Maybe it would be better if she found a secluded spot outside the sweat lodge. Sleep seemed unlikely, given all the commotion. With that in mind, Megan stumbled toward the door, so weary her bones ached.

Jed burst into the room, followed by Bron and Terin. On her feet in an instant, Alice hurtled toward her mates. Jed's arms closed around her, so did Bron's and Terin's.

Les. Karl. Where are they?

For one awful moment, she imagined something hideous had happened. They must've had a battle royale on their hands to be gone for so long. She detoured around Jed and Alice, intent on pushing her way outside. She had to see if her mates were all right. Where were the other injured shifters? Hadn't they been able to extricate them?

"Careful," Les' voice sounded from the other side of the hides. He appeared seconds later carrying one end of a litter. Karl had the other end. She wanted to throw herself into their arms, but it would have to wait. Both men grinned at her. She grinned back just before she dissolved into tears.

Sara let out a whoop and launched herself at the man on the litter, driving it to the ground. She hugged her mate, strung kisses down his face, and crooned to him in Cree. Megan felt happy for her. In the brief time since they'd met, she'd developed respect for the taciturn woman.

And then Les and Karl's arms closed around her. "You're safe," she snuffled through her tears. "Safe. I couldn't let myself think about losing you."

"Yes, and we saved both of Sara's mates. Julaika's too." Karl sounded proud of his pack. She didn't blame him. They'd tackled the gates of Hell and emerged victorious.

"Aw, we're pretty tough to get shut of. You were never in any danger of losing us. I'm filthy and I stink, but I'm going to kiss you anyway." Les closed his mouth over hers. She wound her arms around him and held on for dear life. Karl put his arms around both of them, and she turned her head so she could kiss him.

"Your face." Karl drew back and traced a finger over her bruised jaw.

"And her neck." Les touched it gingerly. "Jesus! That animal hit you?"

She bit her lip and nodded. "It's all right. He could've done worse."

Les growled low in his throat and drew her to him. Karl tightened his hold on her too. Megan basked in her mates' love and caring. What amazing men. The horror from McCollum would recede, but she'd have Les and Karl by her side forever.

"We need to leave before it gets much lighter," Les said.

"Where are we going?"

"The reason Jed didn't roust Alice out again," Karl added, "was we picked up both the Chrysler and the truck once we were done freeing Sara's men. Both vehicles are outside."

Megan drew away from them and placed her hands on her hips. "You didn't answer my question."

"We have to put some distance between us and Red Deer," Les explained. "We killed McCollum—"

"I'm glad," she cut in. "Delighted." And then what it meant sank in and fear knifed her in the gut, turning her insides to mush. She clutched both their arms. "Oh my God, we do need to leave. He was a cop."

Karl nodded. "Yes, and we killed two more civilians. Hunters, but still respected community members."

"Of course no one knows it was us," Les clarified, "because there were no witnesses, but we still need to go."

"Aw, crap!" She looked from one of her mates to the other. "We can't leave until the courthouse opens. I need my passport."

"Not to worry, darling, we have everything," Karl hooked an arm through hers. "We picked it up yesterday along with ours."

A warm glow started in her belly and melted her all the way to the tips of her toes. Being taken care of was a novel experience, but Megan was certain she could get used to it.

"We're leaving the truck here for our friends," Les said and gave her a little push beneath the buffalo hides. "They can use it until we show up again."

"If we never get back this way," Karl added, "it turns from a loan to a permanent gift."

Megan walked out into a damp dawn and stared at the shiny, dove-colored Chrysler sitting just behind Alice's Ford. It glistened with raindrops. "That's the new car?" She pointed.

"That's it, sweetheart." Karl grabbed her hand. "Do you like it?"

"I love it." She turned and glanced back at the sweat lodge. Jed, Alice, Bron, Terin, and the other shifters were just leaving. Megan thought about Julaika and Sara. She owed them a lot. "Do I have time to say good-bye?"

Les and Karl exchanged glances. "Make it fast. We'll get the engine going."

The women must've divined her intent because they met her just inside the doorway. "You've got to leave. Hurry." Sara made shooing motions with both hands.

"Thank both of you so much." Megan kissed them. "I'll visit—"

Julaika shook her head. "Not a good idea, but we are sisters under the skin even if we never see each other again. Sara is right. Go."

"You can be across the border before the sun sets." Sara squeezed Megan's hand. "Once you're in the States, you'll be safer."

"Thank you again. For everything. "Megan spun and sprinted through the rain for the Chrysler. Les was behind the wheel, and Karl held the door for her. She dove into the front seat, ecstatic to be between her mates again. Karl slammed the door, and they headed south.

"We'll take back roads until we clear Red Deer," Les said.

"Maybe once we're south of Calgary, we can get a motel and clean up," Karl added.

"Way south of Calgary," Megan said. "I haven't been gone all that long. The cult is probably still after me."

"We'll let Jed know when we stop for fuel," Les said. "He should be right ahead of us once we hit the main highway."

"I thought Bron and Terin were going to stay in Canada. And what about the clan meeting tonight?" Megan leaned into Les and then into Karl. Les had been right when he said they were filthy, but it felt so good to have them by her side again, she didn't care.

"After last night, Jed rethought his plans. Better to have everyone safe. Our kin here will make sure all the shifters in this region know about the next gathering." Karl arranged an arm behind her back and pulled her against him.

As he often did, Les picked up the conversational thread from his pack mate. "The shifters who helped last night will spread the word throughout Canada. Everyone who can make it will meet up next month at the full moon."

"In the States?" Megan quirked a brow.

Les nodded. "There's a secret meeting place in the High Sierra, not too far from where Jed, Bron, and Terin met Alice for the first time."

~

IT WAS CLOSING on dinnertime when they pulled into Browning, Montana, the bustling center of a huge Blackfoot Indian reservation. Rain dogged them for most of the journey, but it had finally stopped. The three hundred twenty-five miles had taken all day because the roads hadn't been all that smooth, and they'd stopped frequently so Les and Karl could switch drivers. They'd also stopped at a farmer's market on the outskirts of Calgary to stock up on edibles. Both men were exhausted. One dozed, leaning against Megan, while the other drove. She'd offered to drive, but her mates had demurred, telling her she needed practice somewhere other than a highway where the other cars traveled as fast as fifty miles an hour and whooshed past slower vehicles with uncomfortably narrow margins.

She'd worried herself nearly sick about the border crossing, but it turned out to be trivial. Once the customs agent had discovered Jed and Terin worked for Paramount Studios, he'd engaged them in a spirited dialogue about movies and simply waved Megan, Les, and Karl through after cursory glances at their passports.

"Where are we going to stop?" Megan asked. She was tired too, but had managed some sleep along with whichever of her mates wasn't behind the wheel.

"Not much farther." Les smiled encouragingly. "According to Jed, there's a deserted hunting camp just south of town. Guess there used to be a small motel and eatery, but they're closed."

"What? Are we going to break in?" Megan repositioned herself.

She felt sticky and wanted a shower and a hot meal and her mates in her bed.

"No, silly." Les poked her side. "Jed knows the tribal leaders here. He's going to stop and get the keys."

"Yeah, we only break the law if there's not any other choice," Karl said archly and cranked the wheel hard left. "I'm pretty sure this has to be it. We left the bulk of the town half a mile back, and it's the first side road I've seen."

Les craned his neck and peered out the windshield. "There's the sign." He pointed at painted boards nearly overgrown by blackberry bushes. "I'll be glad to get out of the car for a while."

"You and me both, brother." Karl ferried the car into a clearing with several cabins. Slowing, he brought it to a stop.

"It's a whole lot farther than this to California." Megan crawled out after Les. Karl slid from behind the wheel.

"True." Karl sucked in a breath and stood on his tiptoes to stretch. "But we don't have to hurry now that we're across the border."

"It probably would've been fewer miles overall if we'd angled west and come out at Bonner's Ferry, Idaho," Les said. "But we wanted the fastest route out of Canada." He cocked his head to one side. "I hear the other car. Great!"

Alice's Ford rolled to a halt next to the Chrysler. No longer at the wheel, Jed jumped out the passenger door, keys dangling from one hand. He eyed Les and Karl and smacked his lips lasciviously. "How much is it worth to you to have me open a cabin? I know you're champing at the bit to get that new mate of yours in bed."

Alice trotted to his side and punched him in the arm. "Stop it!" Her voice rang with mock severity. "How would you have felt if someone did that when all of us were newly mated?"

"It's okay." Karl spread his arms expansively. "We know he's teasing. Any cabin will do. Just hurry, would you?"

A warm smile lit Jed's face. He turned and strode to the furthermost cabin. Unlocking the door, he pushed it open with a flourish. "It's the honeymoon suite," he announced. "The only one with running water and a stove to heat it."

"We'll take it." Les took one of Megan's hands and Karl the other. Together, they walked up the steps.

Jed hugged each of them. He made an intensely male sound deep in his throat. "We have several long days on the road ahead of us. Plus all of you need to stop at the first big town long enough to buy new clothes. Be sure to get at least some sleep." Breaking into gales of laughter, he ran down the steps and herded Alice and his lieutenants toward a cabin on the far side of the clearing.

Megan let go of her mates and moved inside. Constructed of good-sized logs, the cottage was surprisingly cozy. Chairs and a table sat near one wall not far from a sink and pump handle. A pot-bellied stove squatted in the middle of the room with wooden chairs and a sofa with moth-eaten cushions arranged around it. She walked to a door at the rear of the structure and opened it to find a small room with a double bed that took up nearly all the floor space. She patted the coverlet. Dust flew everywhere, but when she peeled it back, the sheets looked clean enough. Just looking at the bed made her thighs twitch. She rubbed them together, her swollen labia contracted, and she almost came.

Enough of this. The sooner we all get cleaned up, the sooner that bed can see some action.

She returned to the main room but left the bedroom open, so the woodstove could warm it.

Les knelt by the cold hearth, picked up a small ax, and proceeded to shave tinder. "Hey, Karl, bring in some more wood."

The other shifter groaned. "Can't we have a little appetizer first? My dick's so hard it aches."

Megan had been wondering the same thing. The men had rubbed her to several climaxes in the car, and she'd jacked them too, but hunger for her mates ran through her veins like molten lava.

"You think I'm not in the same shape?" Les let go of the ax long enough to pat the front of his belled out pants. "We're all going to clean up first. I can still smell Hunter blood on us. You and I can hit the creek, but we're heating water for our mate."

"No way." Megan dragged the cast iron kettle from off the stovetop and over to the pump. "Now that you mention it, I catch a whiff of McCollum every so often. I'd like to scrub every last trace of that scum off me, but I'm not going to be being separated from you for even the time a cold creek bath would take. We'll wash each other."

"I'm all for that." Karl winked broadly. "It'll be like foreplay. Back in a flash with wood to keep us warm."

CHAPTER 16

The cabin toasted up nicely from the heat of the woodstove. The men had shucked their clothes as soon as the cabin began to warm. Their filthy pants and shirts were soaking in detergent in the kitchen sink. They'd found a galvanized metal bathtub on the back porch and filled it with steaming water.

Les' hands trembled as he and Karl gently undressed Megan, adding her clothes to the ones in the sink as they removed them. Karl unzipped her skirt. Les helped her step out of it and just gaped at her. No matter how many times he saw her naked body, the sight still stole his breath away. What an amazingly gorgeous woman. Hair fell to her waist in golden sheaves, and her blue eyes sparkled with merriment and desire. Full breasts rode high on her ribcage. A slender waist flared to lush hips and long, shapely legs. Blonde curls between her legs beckoned alluringly.

As if she read his mind, she parted her thighs and thrust her hips toward him. Les groaned. "Let's get you into the tub."

"I'll be a frosted monkey if we manage to get through all three baths without attacking each other." Karl palmed the erection jutting out from his body.

Megan's nipples were hard peaks, and her fair skin was splotched with desire. Les took one of her hands, and Karl spanned her waist as both men guided her over the high lip and into the tub. She sank into the water, moaning with pleasure as it closed over her body. She reached for the soap, but Karl beat her to it. He wet the unevenly shaped bar and ran it over her body.

Les grabbed a washrag and followed the soap, sluicing water down their mate's perfect form. He knelt by the tub and took one of her nipples in his mouth. Karl slid a hand between her legs. Megan writhed between them, panting and thrashing. Water slopped over the sides of the tub.

"She's really close." Karl's voice was raspy. "You should feel how tight she is. Her pussy's caught my fingers so hard, I may never get them back. Suck harder."

Les did him one better. He took Megan's other nipple between his fingers and twirled it and then closed his mouth over hers and kissed her deeply. Her body thrummed and bowed between him and Karl, and he knew she was coming. Her arousal thrilled him. His cock rubbed against the side of the warm metal tub, and then her fingers closed around him and he was coming too, shooting jets of hot semen onto the cabin's wood floor.

Megan broke away from their kiss. Letting go of him, she beckoned to Karl. At first he shook his head. "Aw, darling. I'm still filthy."

"I brought you off in the car. You're not any dirtier now than you were then. Come here."

Karl groaned. He moved his hand from between her legs and positioned himself so she could curve her fingers around his erection. Les felt his pack mate's heat. He dropped a hand to his still-throbbing cock and linked to Karl, feeling Megan's firm strokes as she stroked his near-to-bursting penis.

Les covered Megan's mouth with his. The sound of Karl's ragged breathing escalated, and then he cried out as release took him. Les' balls tightened too. For a moment, he thought he might join his pack mate, but then the intensity receded. *Good.* He needed to save something for when they finally got into bed together.

"All right!" Megan managed between panting breaths. "Now let's see if we can't finish this bath project so we can do more than rubbing. Your dicks are so incredible, I want them inside me, not in my hand."

"You heard the lady." Karl laughed, and the sound held a sated, satisfied man edge.

"Can we help you wash your hair?" Les dragged the wet ends of Megan's tresses into a bundle behind her.

"Sure." She grinned. "Let me undo the rest of my braid, first. I'll soap. If you could rinse with fresh water from the kettle, it would be great."

~

"W E COULD START WITH CLEAN WATER." Megan ran a hand through bathwater that had developed a grayish hue after hers and Karl's baths. She wanted her mates with an ache so fierce it clouded her mind and set fire to all her nerves, but she loved both of them and the water really was a murky mess.

Les snorted. "Hey, I'm the original cold shower Charley, remember? Anytime I have warm water, it feels decadent. We can scoop some of this out, I'll kneel in the tub, and you can just pour warm from the kettle over me once I've soaped up."

"Maybe I can use some of the water to rinse the clothes," Megan said. "We need to get them wrung out and hanging near the stove, or we won't have anything to wear tomorrow."

Somehow, all of them ended up squeaky clean standing in small puddles of water, with their clothes hanging on nearby furniture. There'd been plenty of towels in a dusty cabinet. Megan unwound one from her hair and chucked it onto their pile of discards. She glanced at her mates, who were drying themselves.

"I don't think I'll ever get tired of looking at either of you." She twirled, wriggled her fanny, and began a slow, sashaying stroll toward the bedroom.

As she'd expected, Les and Karl nearly pounced on her. The heat of them, one on each side, practically undid her. She wanted to sink to the floor, open her legs, and let first one and then the other sink deep inside. With enormous self-discipline, she made herself walk the final few feet to the bed.

Arms closed around her from all sides. She sank into her mates' embrace, kissing first one and then the other. The feel of their nakedness against her was enticing, full of promise. She dropped her hands and circled a penis with each, stroking with the firm, slow strokes she knew they liked. The men herded her to lie down. She broke away from Karl's lips pressed against hers.

"Got to get the quilt out of the way. It's really dusty."

Les pivoted, made a grab for it, and chucked it onto the floor. A cloud of dust rose and Megan laughed. Men! She would've folded it, but what difference did it make?

"You can civilize us later." Les growled, having obviously intuited her thoughts.

"I'm not sure I want you any more civilized than you already are." She grinned and tossed herself onto the bed. The men lay on both sides, touching, kissing, stroking. Heat built in her loins, urgent and pressing. Her earlier climax hadn't diminished her lust one whit.

"I love you." Les twirled lazy fingers around her stiff nipples.

"So do I." Karl's fingers were busy between her legs.

Warmth, tenderness, and yearning rocked her to her soul. She twined her arms around her mates. "I love both of you, beyond wisdom and reason, probably." Her hips bucked. "And I need you."

Les rolled onto an elbow, his green eyes ablaze with something wild and untamed. "Tell us what you want, darling." He thrust his hips against her side, and the swell of his hard-on pressed into her.

What do I want?

And then she knew. Having both her mates at the same time was the ultimate high. She'd been considering who she wanted inside her first, but this was much better.

"We can do that." Karl must've been in her mind.

"More than can." Les brushed a knuckle over her kiss-swollen lips. "We'd love to."

Megan wriggled to a sit. "How about we trade off? Karl can be inside my pussy and…"

"Your wish is our command. I can hardly wait." Karl's voice was thick with need. He worked his way to the head of the bed and sat with his back against the wall. Firm hands settled on her hips and guided her as she straddled him and sank onto his cock. Sensation shot through her, so intense she wanted to shriek. Her nipples rubbed against his chest, and she rotated her pelvis to maximize contact with her sensitive nub against his pubic bone.

"Ready for me?" The bed creaked as Les knelt behind them. He reached between her legs and slid his fingers around the base of Karl's cock until they reached her clit. He rubbed her a few times, just enough to tease and then trailed his fingers between her ass cheeks, probing the bud of her anus. Her hips bucked back. She wanted him inside, not just diddling her entrance.

And then she felt his cockhead pressing against her rear opening. Megan moved her hips in a circle and felt an inch of him slip inside. He must've slathered her lubrication on his cock because it felt velvety as it continued to move slowly inside her.

The same sharp intensity filled Megan as two cocks plumbed her. Every direction she moved, a fresh jolt of pleasure seared her. Karl moved a hand between her legs and rubbed her clit. Heat swirled in her belly and spewed out. Her pussy convulsed around Karl's cock and her anus clutched Les' as she came.

Karl kissed her, tongue sinking into her mouth. His touch on her sensitive nub backed off, but then he laid a finger on either side and twiddled her clit between them. A second climax roared out of nowhere, snaring her in its grip. Somewhere in the midst of it, she felt both cocks release inside her, juddering hard.

A long time later, Les withdrew, and Karl helped her off him. They lay curled together on the bed. "Sleep, darling." Les draped an arm around her.

"Until one of you wakes me for another round," she murmured. "Not that I'm complaining, mind you."

"Hear that?" Karl said, sounding deeply pleased. "She's not tired of us yet."

"No, but if we do have more sex, I need to clean up a bit." Les levered himself off the bed and walked from the room. She drowsed against Karl until Les returned and gathered her close, cradling her between them. "Now about being tired of us…"

She smiled sleepily. "I'll never get tired of you. How long will it take to get to California?"

"Hmmm… Maybe a week," Les said. "It's over a thousand miles."

"Only a week," she echoed. "Hope we don't make fools of ourselves once we get to Jed's. I suspect we'll retire to our bedroom and not surface for days."

"He'll understand." Karl smoothed hair back from her face.

She thought about the things Alice had told her. "Yeah," she agreed. "They all will, plus I'm looking forward to getting to know Alice better."

Sandwiched between her mates, feeling safe and loved, Megan let sleep take her. She had a whole new life ahead of her, and she was looking forward to every minute of it.

EPILOGUE

It had been closer to fourteen hundred miles between northern Montana and Los Angeles. Megan still couldn't believe the variety of things she'd seen during the week and a half they spent on the road. Many byways had been dirt, and the ones through the Rockies and around the southern end of the Sierras were single lane and very windy. The men let her drive on the straighter stretches, and she was feeling much more competent behind the wheel. It had gotten progressively warmer as they traveled south. The winter clothes she'd purchased in Montana were packed in suitcases in the trunk, and she'd replaced them with lighter fare she picked up when they detoured through Salt Lake City.

They'd stopped in Las Vegas for a night. All the fancy casinos made her jaw drop. The men had taken her to a floor show with scantily clad dancers and free flowing liquor. It was so different from the life she'd left, it was hard to fathom they were still in North America. She'd known Canada was a poor country in comparison with the United States, but now she had some idea what that actually meant. Money flowed freely south of the Canadian border. She saw it in substantial houses and huge farming operations. And in the gambling establishments in Vegas.

"Penny for your thoughts, sweetheart." Les glanced at her from where he sat behind the wheel.

"We're almost there, huh?"

"Sure are." Karl grinned. "All these buildings we're passing must be the northeastern outskirts of Los Angeles."

"It's a whole lot more built up than I was expecting." Les flexed his fingers around the steering wheel.

Alice's Ford pulled around them and honked just before she signaled a right hand turn.

Les fell in behind her. "Guess Alice knows the way."

"Why wouldn't she?" Megan defended her friend. "It's her house too."

"He didn't mean anything by it." Karl draped an arm around her shoulders and pulled her close. "We've known Jed for hundreds of years—"

"And we're delighted he and Bron and Terin finally found a mate," Les added. "It's just going to take a little doing to think of all of them together because the men were alone so long."

"Oh my God." Megan pointed out the open window. "Is that an orange tree?"

"Sure looks like it," Karl said.

She leaned across him and nearly fell out the window staring as they drove past. "There are two, no make that three, of them. Hundreds of oranges. Sure is nice that it's warm here. Is it ever winter this far south?"

"I'm not sure," Les answered.

"We'll have to ask Jed," Karl said.

They drove in silence for the next half hour or so, winding their way deeper into what had to be metropolitan Los Angeles. Between huge buildings and richly clad men and women walking the streets, Megan couldn't decide what to look at first.

Alice turned off the main roadway, and they followed her. Gradually, the streets climbed into hills above the city. "My God. Look at all these huge houses." Megan tried to corral her enthusiasm, but she practically bounced in the seat between the men as she craned her neck looking out the windows. "I swear, they just keep getting bigger."

"I'm sure Jed's house is a showplace," Les said. "He liked nice things in the Old Country too."

"So did the two of you," she countered. "You told me about your castles and servants and the way you lived there."

"So we did." Karl's voice took on a wistful note. "We used to live far more elaborately than we do now, even in Canada, but it didn't seem wise with Hunters on the prowl."

"Is having a big house important to you?" Les asked. He cranked the wheel hard left and followed the Ford into a driveway lined with flowering shrubs.

Megan considered his question. "I don't think so. After all, I lived in a one bedroom apartment, and I was happy there. It's just that all this opulence is…seductive. And overwhelming."

Karl laughed. "I suppose that's one word for it. Wait until you see the inside of Jed's house. We've never been here, but I remember his manor house in Germany."

"Don't forget the castle in Switzerland," Les cut in.

Karl pushed the door open and extended a hand to help Megan. Alice trotted over to them. "We're finally here! I'm so glad we decided to do this, and the drive wasn't really all that bad."

"Not bad at all." Megan smiled. "It was a grand adventure. Biggest one I've ever had. I'm still reeling and trying to pigeonhole everything we saw."

Les got out of the car and joined them. He held out his arms, and Megan walked into them. "Your adventures are just beginning. Karl and I will make sure every single one of your wishes comes true."

Megan hugged him and felt Karl's arms close around her back. She loved how she felt sandwiched between her mates. "You already have," she murmured.

Jed loped to Alice and kissed her long and deep. Bron joined them and turned Alice's head so she could kiss him. Terin clapped his hands together. "Come on, people. We're in the driveway for chrissakes. Let's move the show inside before someone drives past and labels us a bunch of perverts."

"Told you we should've put that wood slat fence up," Jed muttered. He glanced at everyone. "Terin's right, though. I'm not being much of a host. Come on. I'd like to show you the house and figure out which suite you'll want to settle in."

"Do you really have a swimming pool in the basement?" Megan asked. She felt foolish, but she wanted to know.

Jed nodded. "You bet we do."

"What?" Alice punched her arm lightly. "You didn't believe me?"

"Not so much that. It just seemed impossible. I've never even seen an outdoor swimming pool."

"Well—" Jed winked "—you'll see this one soon enough."

Terin made a come along gesture with both hands. "Let's go. We can haul the luggage up later. I'm hungry—and thirsty. We need to break out some of that wonderful old Cabernet and the Irish whiskey too."

"Single malt Scotch for me," Jed said.

Megan grasped her mates' hands. Together they followed Jed, Alice, and the boys up a walkway paved with colored concrete and lined with a variety of lush plants, many with blossoms. "I can't get over that plants bloom all year round here."

"It never gets very cold," Alice called over a shoulder.

"I noticed." Megan wished she'd opted for a sleeveless top. Even her short-sleeved blouse felt too warm, but to be less covered felt immodest.

"Here we go!" Jed pulled a key from one of his many pockets and unlocked the front door. Giving it a push, he walked through, followed by his lieutenants and their mate.

Suddenly shy, Megan held back. Les and Karl tugged at her hands.

"Come on, darling," Les murmured. "It's only a house."

She put one foot in front of the other, walked across the threshold, and stopped dead. Her mouth fell open, and she sucked air like a landed fish. Her gaze rocketed around the room taking in polished wood, priceless antiques, Oriental rugs, and tasteful furniture. Crystal chandeliers hung from several places in the great room's ceiling.

Alice laughed. "Yeah. It had the same impact on me when I first saw it. I thought I'd stumbled into a museum. It was hard to wrap my mind around actually living here."

"B-but you got used to it?" Megan stammered, finding her voice.

"Faster than I ever would have guessed." Alice shrugged. "Not sure what that says about my values. I lived in a very modest house. Same one I grew up in, actually. It was always plenty good enough for me, but if I was honest, I'd have a hard time going back there now."

"You can't, sweetheart." Jed hugged her. "Remember, we sold it."

"So we did."

Jed beamed at everyone. "Les, Karl, Megan, it's my pleasure to have all of you here. I know you probably don't believe me, but you can stay as long as you'd like. If you settled here forever, we'd be honored to share our home."

"How about this?" Bron suggested. "I'll get some food and drink on board." He shot Terin a look. "You can help me."

"Teamwork! I like it!" Jed rubbed his hands together. "Alice and I will give Megan and her mates a tour of the house, so they can decide where they'd like to settle." He eyed them sternly.

"You have to share a meal with us before you retire to your bedroom."

Les snorted. Karl laughed and said, "Humph. Guess you think you won't see us for a while after that."

Alice hooted. "I know we won't. All the bedrooms are just up this stairway. Follow me."

Megan followed along, clinging to her mates. The house was so grand and so impeccably furnished, everything stole her breath away. Just when she thought she'd seen the most perfect sculpture imaginable, she spied another that was even better. The same with paintings. After wandering through all the possible suites, she and her mates decided on a modest affair located on the third floor. It looked out onto gardens. A small porch sported a spiral staircase, which led down to a lovely patio just off the morning room on the main floor.

Jed and Alice tried to convince them to pick something more elaborate, but she and Les and Karl stood firm. They liked the two-bedroom suite with its adjoining bath and claw-foot tub. They'd use one of the bedrooms for a study.

"We can move a bigger bed in," Jed offered.

"We don't need one," Les said. "We slept together in something smaller than this in the cabin, and it worked just fine."

"Well—" Alice quirked a brow "—if you're sure..."

Megan smiled. "We are. If we decide we'd like to change to that bigger room, you'll be the first to know."

"I'll go grab a suitcase or two." Karl turned for the door.

"I'll join you." Les started for the hallway too. "That way we might get everything in one trip."

Alice nuzzled Jed's neck. "How about if you help Bron and Terin?"

"Sure, sweetheart. It will give you a spot of time alone with your friend."

"Exactly." Alice made a grab for his ass as he followed after Les and Karl.

"Watch it!" Jed turned and smirked. "I do crazy things when you touch me, woman."

Megan giggled. Alice joined in and shut the door behind Jed's retreating form. She faced Megan.

"Is this really all right?"

"Oh my." Megan's face heated. "It's so much more than all right, I don't know what to say."

Alice gripped her hand. "Jed and the boys want this to work out. So do I, but probably for different reasons. I'm so looking forward to us being friends."

"Me too." Megan took a chance since she was usually reticent asking personal questions. "Do you know why it's important to Jed and them?"

Alice's smile faded, replaced by a solemn expression. "They're afraid the problem with Hunters will heat up even more. After you were kidnapped, they want to make sure there's enough of them that one of the men is always with us."

"But you have a job. How's that going to work?"

Alice nodded. "Jed wants me to quit. I'm not ready to do that, so the compromise is one of them will drive me there and pick me up every day."

"Are you considering quitting?"

Alice drew her black brows together. "Never thought I'd say this, but yes. I don't want to jeopardize everyone's safety by making the men split up to ferry me back and forth. Jed and Terin and Bron all have jobs, and they're talking about quitting too."

Megan let go of Alice and sank onto the bed. "So all this wonderfulness—" she spread her arms wide "—is bittersweet. I guess I thought once I was away from the cult and we escaped from Red Deer, our problems would get smaller."

"They may. None of us knows." Alice joined her on the bed. "Look at me. What we have with our mates is special. I value each moment I have with Jed and Bron and Terin."

Megan nodded. "I know what you mean. I still can't believe how I feel inside when Les and Karl both hold me."

Alice's mouth curved into a soft smile. "That part will only get better as the mate bond strengthens. Love your mates, cherish them, and try to believe we'll triumph in the end."

"Better us than Hunters like Justin," Megan muttered.

"No shit." Alice cocked her head to one side. "It's Jed. I hear him in my mind. Food's ready."

Footsteps sounded in the hall, and the door swung open. Les staggered into the room beneath an obscenely high pile of bags and suitcases. Similarly burdened, Karl was right behind.

"Wow!" Megan eyed the mountain of their belongings. "We left Canada with nothing. It's almost impossible to believe we bought that much."

"Believe it, darling." Les kissed her cheek once he'd set everything down. "Jed said to join them in the kitchen."

"We already know." Megan kissed him and then Karl.

"Come on!" Alice grinned. "I'm hungry, plus I want to be the first to show Megan the kitchen. She'll appreciate it much more than I did."

Les placed an arm around her waist, and Karl circled her shoulders with one of his. Together, they followed Alice down thickly carpeted stairs, through the great room, and into a huge, old-fashioned country kitchen.

Megan eyed the immense gas range, what had to be a state-of-the-art refrigerator, and gleaming rows of pots and pans. She squealed. "I actually get to cook in here?"

"We'd be most appreciative," Bron and Terin said with one voice from where they sat at a carved oak table beneath a window.

"Gee, thanks," Alice mumbled. "I know cooking's not my strong suit, but you could sound a little less enthusiastic."

"Aw, honey." Bron vaulted to his feet, hurried across the

kitchen, and drew her into a hug. "It's just that we got a taste of Megan's cooking at the cabin."

Alice's stern expression dissolved into chortles. "Yeah. So did I. What are you all waiting for?" She followed Bron to the table where plates of cheese and cold cuts were laid out.

Les led Megan to a chair, and Karl filled a plate for her. Jed took charge of drinks. She didn't realize how hungry she was until she started eating. They'd had breakfast that morning but no lunch, and it was almost dinnertime. After eating nonstop for a few minutes, she looked up. "I want to thank all of you."

"Aw, you don't have to thank us, sweetheart—" Les turned his head and kissed her cheek.

She wriggled away. "No, but I want to. I'm so in love with you and Karl, it warms me all the way to my toes. And I'm grateful to Alice and Jed and Bron and Terin for offering us our first real home."

Les' brows drew together, but she laid a hand over his mouth. "The cabin has possibilities, and maybe we'll go back there to explore them, but we had to leave after you rescued the shifters and killed three Hunters."

"She's right." Karl kissed her other cheek. "Thanks, Jed, for offering us shelter."

"We do appreciate it," Les cut it. "Really, we do. And we stand ready to do whatever we have to, so we'll be more than dead weight around here."

"Thanks. I already know what hard workers you are." Worry flickered behind Jed's blue eyes. "It's good there are more of us to keep the women safe."

"Let's not go there," Alice said. "Let's take today for what it is and celebrate getting home and being together."

"I'll drink to that." Megan raised her glass.

The men did the same. Amidst murmurs of good wishes, they all drank a toast to today and the wonder of the love flowing among them.

This is the end of book two of Wolf Clan Shifters. Look for the next one, *Sophie's Shifters*, very soon. Storm clouds are piling up on the horizon, and the shifters gather only to face a devastating attack. A sample follows.

ABOUT THE AUTHOR

Ann Gimpel is a national bestselling author. A lifelong aficionado of the unusual, she began writing speculative fiction a few years ago. Since then her short fiction has appeared in a number of webzines and anthologies. Her longer books run the gamut from urban fantasy to paranormal romance. Once upon a time, she nurtured clients. Now she nurtures dark, gritty fantasy stories that push hard against reality. When she's not writing, she's in the backcountry getting down and dirty with her camera. She's published over 50 books to date, with several more planned for 2018 and beyond. A husband, grown children, grandchildren and wolf hybrids round out her family.

Keep up with her at www.anngimpel.com or http://anngimpel.blogspot.com

If you enjoyed what you read, get in line for special offers and pre-release special reads. Sign up for Ann's newsletter on her website or her blog.

SOPHIE'S SHIFTERS

Jed Starnes, the wolf shifter clan's alpha, made a concerted effort to unclench his jaw. He scanned the hundreds of shifters—wolf, bear, coyote, and mountain cat—assembled in a cave deep in the High Sierra and itched to shake sense into every last one of them. Gritty dust from the cave's dirt floor made his eyes feel scratchy—or maybe it was a result of three straight days of arguing. Everyone was on edge, and several shifters were engaged in a shouting match. He'd called them off earlier, but they were back at each other's throats again.

"This isn't working." Keir, clan alpha for bears, sat on Jed's right and spoke low into his ear. A tall, powerfully built man with thick, shaggy black hair and a weather-beaten face, he skewered Jed with shrewd dark eyes.

"No shit. What do you want to do about it?"

"Call a break for an hour. Send everyone outside to cool off—"

"Goddammit!" Jed lunged to his feet. Several of the men had shifted and mountain cats stood with their hackles raised, facing off against a pack of coyotes.

"Do something about your men," Keir snarled at Blake, alpha for coyotes.

Jon, alpha for mountain cats jumped in quickly. "Your pack started it," he told Blake.

"In a pig's eye they did." Blake, tall and slender, shot to his feet and raced between the snarling groups of animals. Long, blond hair was tied into a queue low on his neck, and his blue-green eyes looked deadly.

"Fuck! If he's there, I have to be too." Jon raced after Blake, screeching at his men to take their human forms. Strongly built, like the cat he turned into, his legs and arms pumped as he began throwing punches right into mountain cat snouts. His red-streaked dark hair whipped around him, and Jed imagined his dark eyes were scrunched in anger.

Jed turned to Keir, who stood next to him, a look of concern stamped into his rough features. "We can't just turn our boys loose to kill Hunters and humans."

"I know that," Keir grunted. "Yet I understand why they want to. We're all sick to death of being Hunted, persecuted, and having to hide. You got lucky finding a mate. Me too, but so many of us are alone, and they blame humans for their predicament."

"It runs deeper than the lack of mates," Jed said. "No one enjoys hiding what they are. Our people want to stand proud in the light of day. They're demanding equal rights with humans, and I can't fault them for that."

Keir tilted his chin downward. "Fancy words, wolf man. How do you propose to make something as sweeping as *equal rights* happen?"

"Jesus, but I wish I knew." Jed felt tired, like his limbs were mired in slow-setting concrete. "We need to convince humans we're not a threat. That they can coexist with us. I kept thinking this problem would sort itself out, but it's only gotten worse."

Keir slitted his eyes slyly. "We could help humans—be a resource if they'd let us. We're stronger than they are, and our senses run deeper."

"Look how well that worked in Europe during the war a few

years back. We took our animal forms to protect our allies, and they shot as many of us as they could."

Keir didn't answer with words. One hand morphed into a paw and he dragged his long, curved claws down a wall, leaving deep gouges.

Anger twisted Jed's stomach into a burning knot. He blew out a tense breath as Jon and Blake plodded back to the front of the cave. When he glanced at the shifters, he noted everyone was human again. Aggression still tainted the air, but the frantic edge had lessened.

"Fixed for now," Jon muttered.

"Yeah, but not for long," Blake cut in. "We need to come up with something everyone buys into."

"Not going to be easy." Jed spread his hands in front of him. "Not with a third of the group wanting to kill on sight. That would be suicide—"

"You think they don't know that?" Jon sputtered.

"Desperate times require desperate solutions." Blake nodded once, sharply.

"One solution is for us to simply take our animal forms and remain in them," Keir said thoughtfully. We could blend in with local animal groups, and Hunters wouldn't be able to tell which was which. They only scent us out when we're human."

"What about our mates?" Jed demanded, thinking of Alice, the tall, striking woman mated to him and his two lieutenants, Bron and Terin.

A low growl rattled from the depths of Keir's throat. "Never said it was a perfect solution. Those of us who aren't mated might agree with that strategy."

"I'm not mated," Blake said, "and I think it's badly flawed."

"How so?" Keir bristled.

The coyote shifter shook hair out of his eyes and exhaled raggedly. "Because it's giving up, saying they won, and we'll take whatever scraps the human table chucks our way."

"Fine." Keir lifted his upper lip, showing long incisors. "You come up with something."

"That's the problem in a nutshell." Jed jumped in before they started throwing punches. "If we can't agree, how can we expect our packs to?"

"I'm listening." Jon squatted on his haunches and looked up at Jed.

"We have to draft a staged approach," Jed replied. "Sort of a Plan A, Plan B, and Plan C."

"How?" Keir rumbled. "There'd have to be some pretty clear demarcations telling us when we moved from one to the other. Landmarks that would be obvious to all of us."

"Yeah." Jed crouched next to Jon. "That's always been the stumbling block. It won't help us if coyotes rampage through towns sniffing out Hunters and killing them, while the rest of us are appealing to local political leaders for amnesty."

"Do we know if the Hunters still have ties to the Church?" Blake asked. "They trained the first Hunters, but it seems to me that they wouldn't have needed the Church after that."

"No idea." Jed shook his head. "But a good question."

"Boss!" Terin and Bron skidded to a halt a few feet from Jed, breathing hard.

"Whatever this is better be important." Jed straightened. It took way more effort than it should have.

Terin raked a hand through his long auburn hair and snorted derisively. "You assigned us guard duty."

"Did you forget?" Bron arched his dark brows Jed's way.

"Yes. No. Aw, shit, just say whatever it is you interrupted us for." Jed made an impatient hand gesture. "Then you can get back to watching the mountain scenery. You have the easy job. I'd trade you in a hot second."

Keir waved Jed to silence. "They may be your men, but I bet they're not bringing welcome news."

"Hunters," Bron growled succinctly.

"Lots of them. More than I've ever seen in one place." Usually imperturbable, Terin sounded rattled.

"Define what *more* means." Jon rose to his feet in a single, fluid motion.

Blake moved closer. "How many of those bastards?"

Jed pulled himself together. "Yes. How many and how close?" Depending on what they faced, the choices he hoped they had might be pulled out from under them.

"Half a mile," Bron said.

"Between fifty and sixty. Maybe more than that. We didn't stick around to count them." Terin squeezed his eyes shut for a moment. When he opened them, fury blazed from their amber depths.

"With those numbers," Jon spoke slowly, thoughtfully. "They'd almost have to know we're up here. I've never heard of so many Hunters in one place before."

"What do you think?" Keir stood tall, squaring his shoulders and gazing right at Jed.

"Does it matter?" Jed countered.

"Yes," the bear shifter replied. "We've always governed by democratic principles, and we're not going to stop now."

Terin and Bron looked at Jed expectantly. He knew what his lieutenants wanted. They'd been champing at the bit to kill Hunters for years. He pushed his over-loaded brain into action searching for options, and it kept circling back to the same place. It wasn't that he didn't enjoy killing the sons of bitches who'd targeted them, but he feared retribution that would wipe their kind off the face of the Earth.

"Well?" Blake stared him down with eyes that had shaded to a glittering aquamarine.

"They've backed us into a corner," Jed grunted. "No way that their presence here is accidental. Not with those kinds of numbers."

"We could wipe every single one of those fuckers out." Keir set his mouth in a hard line.

"Sure we can." Jed gritted his teeth together. "I wasn't worried about us prevailing. But what happens then? Surely someone will notice when this many Hunters disappears in the Sierras. They'll send out search parties—probably for years."

Karl and Les, wolf shifters from Canada, trotted close. "Sorry, we were eavesdropping," Karl said, not looking the least bit chagrined. "Why couldn't we do what we did with that posse we killed in Canada?"

"Someone would locate this cave eventually," Jed muttered. "It's not that great a hiding place unless it has some subterranean caverns we haven't stumbled onto yet. Besides, you only hid seven bodies. It's sounding like we'll have ten times that number to dispose of."

"I wasn't thinking of using the cave," Les said. "The Palisade Glacier begins about a thousand feet above us. It's riddled with crevasses. We can dump the bodies into them. That way no one would ever find them."

Hope speared Jed with glass-bright edges so sharp, they were almost painful. There were enough shifters to not only kill, but also set up transport lines to move the dead onto the glacier. "I like it." He clapped Les on the shoulder. "It just might work."

"It will," Blake said. "So long as we don't leave blood trails."

"Clean kills," Jon cut in. "No major vessel severing. Paw swipes across the head and broken neck vertebrae."

"Should keep the bleeding to a minimum." Jed tried to tamp down the savagery boiling up from his guts. He wanted to kill and keep killing as much as any of them. He'd been trying to do what was best for his kin, but holding his aggression at bay had cost him dearly.

"Men!" Keir faced the crowd and waved his arms. "Listen up."

The dull roar of conversation quieted as better than four hundred shifters turned to face the front of the cave.

Jed joined Keir and was flanked by Jon and Blake. The others looked to him as de facto leader of all the clans. He wasn't certain how it had happened, but he straightened his spine and projected his voice, using magic to make certain everyone heard him.

"Somehow Hunters discovered we were meeting. I'm certain they don't have our exact location, but fifty or sixty of them are in the vicinity searching for us."

"Won't be hard," someone called from the middle of the crowd.

"No shit," another man shouted. "They'll smell us."

"Can we kill them?" a third man yelled.

A chant of, "Kill, kill, kill," rose into the air.

Jed shouted. "Quiet. Goddammit. Yes, we're killing them, but listen up. We're going to do it a certain way. Minimal blood. We don't want to leave a track a mile wide for the authorities when they turn these mountains upside down hunting for those fuckers."

"What about the bodies?" someone cried.

"Yeah, what about them?" someone else yelled. "It'd be too disgusting to have to eat them."

"Might be fun," yet another shifter muttered from the sidelines, "so long as they were still alive when we sliced into their guts with our teeth."

"What part of *no blood*, didn't you get?" Blake demanded, sounding pissed.

"Sorry, boss," the coyote shifter grumbled before quieting.

Before the room devolved into yet one more argument, Jed started talking again. "I want a hundred of you to swarm up to the glacier. Identify a few really deep crevasses, and we'll dump the bodies there. Once you've found promising crevasses, form at least two lines so we can move the bodies out of the field and onto the glacier as fast as possible."

"Decide now!" Keir thundered. "Fighters to the left, glacier workers on the right. Two minutes, men. If you haven't sorted yourselves, we'll do it for you."

"Where do you want us?" Bron spoke quietly next to Jed's ear.

"With me, but I need to determine exactly where we'll be."

Jed considered it. He'd just assumed he'd be fighting, and if he fought he wanted his lieutenants by his side, but it made sense for one of the clan leaders to oversee the glacier project. In many ways, obliterating evidence was far more critical than killing.

"I agree." Keir walked up behind Jed. "Sorry, I helped myself to your thoughts. I'll head up the glacier project."

"Excellent." Jed flashed him a grin.

"Move out." Keir bellowed and ran toward the cave's entrance, shucking clothing as he went. "Glacier detail follow me. Shift for now. Easier to travel with four feet than two. Once we get to the glacier, we'll decide if we stay in our animal forms."

As soon as he was done talking, the air around him shimmered brightly, and a shaggy, black bear stepped from the glowing light. The others in his crew followed suit, leaving in a cloud of dust raised by claws digging into the cave's soft, dirt floor.

Jed rounded up Jon and Blake. Together they faced the group. "We're going to stick with the compass points we have an affinity for," Jed informed them. Wolves will follow me, form a group, and take on Hunters approaching from the west."

"Coyotes will cover the east under my direction," Blake said.

"I'll head up mountain cats, and we'll take the southern flank," Jon told the group.

"What about bears?" a shifter asked. "What if there are Hunters from the north?"

"I know you want us with you," Bron said, "but Terin and I can lead the bears—if they'll let us."

"What do you think?" Jed addressed his question to the bear shifters.

"I'm Waldo, one of Keir's lieutenants." A tall, broad-shouldered man with ice blond hair and pale blue eyes stepped forward. "Our other lieutenant is home watching over our mate." He bowed slightly in Bron and Terin's direction. "I welcome your assistance, but I only require one of you."

"Fine." Jed looked from Bron to Terin. "Your idea. You pick who goes with our bear brothers."

"Me." Bron trotted to Waldo's side. "Ready when you are." His dark eyes glittered with bloodlust.

"I've been ready for years." Waldo clapped him on the back. "Let's roll."

Light glistened and shimmered in waves as the men found their animal forms and left the cave. Jed would've appreciated the beauty of their transformative ability if they weren't headed into a full-blown war.

To avoid a bottleneck at the cave's entrance, he let the other groups leave first. When it was down to just wolves, he instructed them to shift before herding them up the ramp that led to the cave's carefully hidden entrance deep in a huge boulder field. Hunter stench hit him dead in the face even before he was fully outside. Good thing they hadn't tarried any longer hammering out the fine points of their attack plan.

He glanced at Terin. *"Ready?"*

"More than ready." He skinned his lips back from his teeth and snarled.

The din of battle rose around them. At least it appeared they wouldn't have to chase down the Hunters. Fighting was all around them. Jed raised his mind voice so everyone could hear him. *"Pick a target. Kill cleanly. No blood. Once one is down, move to the next. Keep going until no Hunters are left."*

"What if the yellow-bellied bastards try to make a run for it?"

Jed raised his muzzle and howled with lupine laughter. *"You're faster. Chase them down. The most important thing is that none of them leave to tell anyone what happened here."*

A chorus of *"Got its,"* flooded his mind, followed by the sharp retort of a rifle blast.

"Move out now!" Jed headed for where the Hunter reek was

thickest with Terin by his side. Bullets flew fast and furious, but shifters had good recuperative powers, unless they took a direct hit to a vital organ.

A small group of Hunters shambled toward them, stumbling over car-sized boulders littering a glacial moraine from when the ice sheet above them had extended much farther east.

Watching them, Jed understood this wouldn't be any kind of contest at all. Their animal forms had far greater agility in rough terrain. *"I'll take the one on the right,"* he told Terin moments before he arced through the air, landing on the Hunter. The man's rifle clattered to the ground, useless, and Jed pounded the side of his head with a powerful paw swipe. He heard vertebrae in the man's neck cracking. For good measure, he hit the man's head from the other direction to the accompaniment of more breaking bones.

Pain flashed into his flank. Snarling, Jed glanced at another Hunter pounding him with a rifle butt. Laughing to himself at how easy this was, Jed reared up and slashed his claws across the man's eyes, blinding him before he broke his neck. He lost count of how many he killed, moving smoothly from one to another. Bloodlust warmed his gut. Sending Hunters straight to Hell was long overdue. He kicked himself for holding his men back this long, and then realized his ability to reason in his wolf form wasn't all that sharp. There'd be a price for today, but by God, every single moment was worth it.

They forced us. They came after us.

We had no choice.

Jed stopped thinking. It cut into the simple joy of dispatching his enemies. The die was cast. There may have been an alternative, but he was damned if he saw it. Hunters would've sniffed out the cave, converged on it, and murdered them if they hadn't fought back.

The occasional animal howl told him some Hunter's rifle had found its mark, but he'd expected a few casualties. He hoped no one would be mortally wounded. Losing even one more of his kin to Hunters was unacceptable.

The sun was moving toward the western horizon when he looked for his next target and couldn't locate anything left to kill. He scrambled to the top of an enormous boulder to scan the field. The sight pleased him. Not only were there no Hunters—except the ones lying on the ground—a smooth operation to move the bodies uphill was underway.

He raised his muzzle and howled. Bron and Terin sprinted to him and climbed the boulder, their claws scrambling for purchase on the slick granite. Because it would make conversation easier, Jed shifted and motioned for his lieutenants to do the same.

"Did we get them all?" he asked once he'd reclaimed his man's body.

"Yup." Bron fist-pumped the air. "Had to chase after about ten who decided they didn't like the odds, but we got them too."

"Any idea how many there were?" Jed asked.

Terin shook his head. "More than we originally thought, but less than a hundred."

"Did all of us respect the minimal blood command?"

"I think so." Bron replied.

Jed cut to the chase. "How about wounded on our side?"

"Not sure, but from where I was fighting, the few of us hit with bullets were able to heal spontaneously," Terin replied.

Jed quirked a brow at Bron. "Same question."

"Everyone knows I'm the best healer we have in all the packs, and no one called for me. That speaks for itself."

Satisfied they'd done the best they could, Jed said, "Let's round up everyone. The more of us helping, the faster we'll get the rest of those bodies out of here."

"What happens then?" Terin asked.

"We go home and lay low," Jed replied. "And hope to hell the powers that be don't launch a witch hunt to smoke us out of our homes."

"I'll rustle up everyone to help," Bron offered. He pointed at groups of shifters cavorting among the rocks, clearly celebrating their victory.

"I'll go with you," Terin said. "It'll go faster with two of us."

"See you on the glacier." Jed scrambled down from the boulder and detoured into the cave to grab his clothes. He didn't really care about them, but he needed his boots to clamber around on the icy glacier. By the time he got there, the work lines were moving the last bodies into crevasses. He inspected the glacier for blood, gratified they hadn't left very much.

As if nature was on their side, a sharp rumble blasted him moments before the cloudy sky let loose. Rain, sleet, and hail pummeled him, but he welcomed it. His hair plastered wetly against his head, and he wiped water from his eyes, but he couldn't stop smiling at their good fortune.

"Son of a bitch." Keir slid to where Jed stood. He was barefoot on the icy surface—and naked. Jed offered him points for being tough. Clearly not uncomfortable in the least, the bears' alpha was grinning like a fool. "Someone up there likes us."

"It certainly appears that way. Beyond that, you did a hell of a good job here." Jed whacked Keir on the back, and the bear shifter cuffed him back playfully.

"It was easy." Keir shrugged off the praise, but he looked pleased. "This glacier has more holes than Swiss cheese. You're the one who thought of it."

"Not me." Jed shook his head. "Les, one of my Canadian kin."

"Regardless." Keir scanned the expanse of ice above them. Water ran down his face and dripped into his eyes. "Think we're about done here."

"Yeah. Sooner we get out of here, the better."

"Boss!" Karl's voice reverberated in his head.

"I'm on the glacier. What is it?"

"Les and I were headed back to make sure we hadn't missed any bodies when we found something."

Keir furled his brows, obviously listening in. *"Whatever it is,"* he chortled, *"kill it."*

"Not sure we want to do that." Les' unmistakable inflection cut in.

"Yeah," Karl seconded. *"It's a woman."*

"What the fuck?" Jed exchanged glances with Keir, who drew his brows into a tight line, looking puzzled.

"We're in the cave," Karl said. *"We think you should come. She's mighty scared, and we need to get her out of here without her pitching a fit."*

"On my way."

Jed had turned to go when Keir clamped a hand around his upper arm. "She's a witness," he hissed. "You do get that?"

"Yeah. I read you loud and clear."

Jed trudged downhill, lost in thought. Killing a woman went against the grain, but they couldn't let her live to reveal today's carnage, either. Cutting out tongues had gone out of style in the Middle Ages, besides that would almost be worse than killing her outright.

"I'll figure it out after I get there and see her," he muttered, reluctant to let anything intrude on today's victory.

www.ingramcontent.com/pod-product-compliance
Lightning Source LLC
Chambersburg PA
CBHW071803190726
48292CB00008B/2694